Masked Reflections

Masked Reflections

DEE STUART

THORNDIKE
CHIVERS

This Large Print edition is published by Thorndike Press®, Waterville, Maine USA and by BBC Audiobooks, Ltd, Bath, England.

Published in 2004 in the U.S. by arrangement with Maureen Moran Agency.

Published in 2004 in the U.K. by arrangement with the author.

U.S. Hardcover 0-7862-6807-7 (Romance)
U.K. Hardcover 1-4056-3053-1 (Chivers Large Print)

The text of this Large Print edition is unabridged.
Other aspects of the book may vary from the original edition.

Set in 16 pt. Plantin by Liana M. Walker.

Printed in the United States on permanent paper.

British Library Cataloguing-in-Publication Data available

Library of Congress Cataloging-in-Publication Data

Stuart, Dee.
  Masked reflections / Dee Stuart.
    p. cm.
  ISBN 0-7862-6807-7 (lg. print : hc : alk. paper)
    1. Mistaken identity — Fiction. 2. Stalking victims — Fiction. 3. Missing persons — Fiction. 4. Colorado — Fiction. 5. Sisters — Fiction. 6. Twins — Fiction. 7. Large type books. I. Title.
  PS3569.T813M37 2004
  813'.54—dc22   2004052849

Dedication

For:

Jane Booras
Sandy Gilbreath
Becky Hensley
Shelia Patterson
Virginia Roberts
Sandra Shurtleff
Gunther Skall
Barbara Stuart
Suzanne Sugalski
Jan Terrell

With many thanks and appreciation for their generous assistance in the preparation of this manuscript.

Chapter One

Once again Kelly Conover tried to stifle the feeling of foreboding that had crept into her heart when Kim hadn't answered her phone — the feeling of dread that had plagued her drive cross-country from New York to Colorado.

Kelly was no stranger to these inexplicable feelings. She and Kim had shared this peculiar rapport since the day they were born, and had later learned to accept it as common to their special bond of twinship. Now Kelly was compelled by more than a mere mood. She was obsessed with the need to see Kim; if Kim didn't answer her phone, something had to be terribly wrong. Time and again she had tried to call her, from home and on the road as well, and had finally sent a telegram to tell Kim she was on her way.

Closer than most sisters, with no other family, they had never lived apart. After Kim accepted a job in Colorado, they kept in touch by letter and phone, once, sometimes twice a week. For the past two weeks there had been no letters from Kim, and no phone calls. Now Kelly was desperate to see her sister, to offer help if necessary, to make sure she was well and happy. With each mile that passed, her excitement and anticipation mounted. She was almost there!

Two miles west of Blue Angel Mountain, Kelly spun the wheel of her white Mustang convertible left and drove slowly down the dirt road where Kim lived. In the thin, pale light of the rising moon, she stared in dismay at the lonely row of brand-new condos stuck on a desolate strip of snow-clad land. Alpine Village was a far cry from what she'd expected. She had envisioned clusters of neat, white, cubelike condos clinging to a hillside within walking distance of the ski town. Instead, she saw an unbroken line of brown Swiss chalets with burnt-orange doors, picture windows, and peaked roofs shrouded with snow. Thick icicles, glistening like long, sharp stilettos, clung to the eaves.

No street lamps shed their bright gleam down the dark street, and only a sprinkling of lights winked from the few condos that were occupied. There was something strange, almost sinister, about the emptiness, the loneliness of the isolated row of chalets, which even the bright spill of moonlight couldn't dispel. But Kim was here, she thought happily, and that was all that mattered.

The beam of Kelly's headlights picked up luminous white numbers painted on the curb. She pulled up before number twelve and pressed hard on the horn, giving a jubilant blast to announce her arrival. No welcoming light appeared, no smiling face was framed in the window. Swiftly she opened the door and slid from the car into the bitter-cold winter night. The hard-packed snow squeaked under her cordovan boots as she strode up the walk, idly thinking how unlike her sister it was to let layers of snow accumulate on the walk.

A broad smile wreathed her face as she jabbed at the bell. Moments slid by. A small coil of uneasiness tightened inside her. Maybe the bell was out of order. She rang again, and heard a faint tinny ring echoing through the house. Time seemed to stop, waiting with her, as she stood shivering on the doorstep. She knocked sharply on the door. As if in reply, she heard the strident jangle of the phone demanding to be answered. "Well, someone expects Kim to be here," Kelly told herself hopefully. The ringing finally died away and endless moments dragged by until it struck her that if Kim wasn't answering the doorbell or phone, it wasn't likely she'd answer her knock.

A wave of disappointment swept through her. Kim was probably working late; maybe she'd gone out for the evening, or maybe she'd come home from work wiped out and was napping. Kim had always slept like the dead. Under her breath Kelly murmured, "If Kim isn't expecting you, if she's not here, it's your own fault. After all, you came two weeks earlier than you'd planned."

But the telegram, persisted a nagging voice. *She should have gotten my telegram!*

Resolutely, Kelly turned from the door, strode back to the car, and eased onto the front seat. In the dim glow of the overhead light, she fished through her beige leather shoulder bag. Thank heaven she'd remembered to bring the house key Kim had sent her the day she moved to Alpine Village. It was taped to a card on which Kim had written in neat, round script: *The door is open, any day, any time. Wish you were here.* Kelly smiled to herself. That was Kim, ever loving, thoughtful, provident. Mournful yowls from the backseat warned her that her cats had had it with cross-country travel.

"Okay, fellas, the excitement's over." Kelly stepped from the car, reached into the backseat, and hauled out a white wicker basket. The yowls grew louder. "Just because I adopted you doesn't mean you can run my life. You're not *my* favorite traveling companions either."

She smiled inwardly. During the exhilarating, passionate, and zany months of her romance with Brad, he had often teased her about her hang-up, taking in strays; he had said the cats knew a pigeon when they saw one. For just a moment she wondered what he was doing — and with whom — and wished she'd taken him up on his offer to keep the cats. But she'd wanted to make a clean break, and had insisted on taking them with her. Brad York was far behind her, and she refused to think of him now. She flipped open the lid of the basket and a jumble of jet-black, calico, and ginger-colored cats scampered out.

She dragged her white leather suitcase from the front seat, picked up the wicker basket, and marched to Kim's front door, then returned to the car and unstrapped her skis and poles from the rack, the cats frisking at her heels.

After opening the door, she set down the skis and poles and dragged the suitcase and

11

basket inside the darkened house. Loudly she called, "Kim? Kim, it's me, Kelly. Where are you?" She heard only a hollow silence as she stood waiting in the darkness. A chill knifed through her. Like a sharp cold blade, it penetrated her cashmere coat, her heavy Harris tweed suit. She took a deep breath, steeling herself against — against what? A twinge of apprehension tingled up her spine. With a defiant toss of her head, she shouted, "Kim Conover! Are you here?" Unbroken silence echoed around her. At least that answers my question, thought Kelly dismally. Obviously she is *not* here.

The chilly chalet had the dank, musty smell of a place that had been closed up for a time, and hulking forms seemed to rise from the shadowy darkness. Her skin crawled. She pulled off her gloves and fumbled for a light switch beside the door. Suddenly the room sprang to life. She let out an astonished gasp, then stood motionless, staring around the light, spacious living room. All the drawers in a built-in desk were pulled out, their contents dumped on the floor. The bookshelves that divided the living room from the dining area were swept clean. Kelly winced at the sight of the thick, tooled leather–covered family Bible, Kim's precious books, and her collection of photographs strewn on the floor. The pictures on the walls all hung askew. A trail of large, muddy footprints crossed the beige carpet. Kelly's stricken gaze traveled upward to a railed loft bedroom under the cathedral ceiling. Was Kim up there lying hurt, unconscious, or worse? Fear closed Kelly's throat. Heart pounding, she raced up the open wooden staircase to the bedroom. As she flicked on the heavy pottery lamp beside the king-size bed, quick relief followed by outrage flooded through her: relief that Kim was not lying there injured — or worse — in her bed; outrage that Kim's home had been invaded, defiled. The armoire doors stood open, Kim's clothes jammed to the sides; nightstand and dresser drawers had been pulled out, and obviously had been rummaged through.

A wry smile twisted Kelly's lips. A burglar couldn't have found much here. Kim owned mostly costume jewelry. Her gaze flew to Kim's petit point–covered jewelry box on top of the dresser. The thief must have known good jewelry when he saw it, or else he'd have taken the box. Odd, though, that he'd bothered to close the lid when he'd left everything else open. Maybe, after finding nothing of value, he had slammed it shut in disgust. She reached out and snapped the catch. Locked! This was odder still. Why hadn't the thief pried it open — or simply taken it with him? Kelly shook her head, thinking she should just be grateful that the box was still here and that Kim hadn't been around when the thief broke in. Or had she? Kim could be in the kitchen. Or in the . . . The thought of what she might still find made her blood run cold.

Kelly raced down the stairs, through the living room, and down a short hall. Passing a doorway leading to a small bathroom, she cast a quick glance beyond a second door which opened onto a cavernous closet. At the end of the hall, she paused in the doorway of what had to be the kitchen, straining to see through the blackness. Her groping fingers found the light switch. She stood motionless, hearing only the sound of her uneven breathing as her gaze raked Kim's cheerful red and white kitchen. Every drawer, every door in the white wooden cabinets stood open except one.

Then she saw it — a sheet of Kim's pale blue stationery, held in place by the sharp, pointed blade of a kitchen knife stuck into the cabinet door. She felt the hairs prickle on the back of her neck. A scream rose in her throat and she clapped her hand over her mouth in horror. As she stood staring at the evil-looking knife anger overrode fear. Furiously she strode to the cabinet, yanked out the knife, and clutched the paper. Her hand shook as her eyes traveled down the page. Bold black letters seemed to leap up at her. *I'm watching for you. When you come back, I'll be waiting.*

Her heart pounded wildly. The police! She must call the police! Why hadn't she called them the minute she walked in the door! She glanced about the kitchen, searching for a phone. There was no phone here! She dashed down the hall to the living room. Her desperate gaze swept past the picture window across the front of the chalet, the TV and stereo in one corner, past the massive stone fireplace dominating the far wall, to the built-in desk. There, in a jumble of papers she spotted a moss green phone.

With trembling fingers she dialed the operator and was put immediately through to the police department. Trying to keep her voice calm and controlled, she reported the break-in. She thought she heard a suppressed sigh, as if the dispatcher had heard the same story a dozen times. She was only slightly reassured when he promised to send someone out at once. Nervously she glanced at her watch. Almost eight. If Kim were working late, she should be home by now. Much as Kelly hated to break the news of a burglary over the phone, Kim had to know. She'd have to tell the police what was missing.

Delving in her purse, she retrieved a small red address book, looked up Kim's phone number at work, and dialed. After two rings, a singsong voice said: "Alpenstock Land Development Corporation. Business hours are from nine to five. Please call again." A recording! Unnerved, Kelly slammed down the receiver.

As she stared around the disheveled room a slightly hysterical laugh escaped her. She must pull herself together, she thought, shivering. She located the thermostat, turned it on, then lugged her suitcase upstairs. Hastily she shrugged off her coat and suit and pulled on a heavy white turtleneck sweater and black woolen slacks. She would unpack later, after the police had seen what a mess the thief had made. She started violently as something brushed against her shins, then felt foolish when Cleo let out a long, mournful wail.

"Okay, Cleo, we'll find some food."

Distraught, Kelly trekked to the kitchen and opened the fridge. Thank heaven there was food inside. She poured some milk into a dish and set it on the floor. Cleo took one sniff, turned up her nose, and began rubbing her sleek furry body against Kelly's legs.

Kelly picked up the dish and sniffed, wrinkling her nose at the acrid odor. She opened the fridge and pulled out a package of bacon. It was stiff and dry. She lifted the lid on a green plastic bowl and drew back. Beans, covered with furry gray mold. She pulled open the vegetable drawer. Inside lay a bunch of broccoli with withered leaves and yellowed flowerets. She ran to the sink, turned on the water, and stuffed the rotted food down the garbage disposal.

Kelly's pale blonde brows drew together in a scowl. Sour milk? Spoiled food? Such things never happened in Kim's house. Uneasy thoughts raced through Kelly's mind. Had Kim gone away unexpectedly? It didn't seem she had just gone out for the evening. The premonitions of trouble that had plagued Kelly from the moment she left New York returned in full measure.

Restlessly she paced the living room, wishing Kim would hurry home. If she'd been on her way home from work when Kelly called, she'd be here by now. With every passing moment, Kelly felt more fidgety. She couldn't endure standing around waiting for something to happen. She lifted the family Bible from the floor and set it on the bookcase, then bent down and picked up a photograph. Dust dimmed the glass. Glancing around the room, she noticed that the desk, and the lamp table, too, were dusty. Kim was an immaculate housekeeper. Was she now too busy to dust? Had she grown careless, living alone? Strange, very strange.

Kelly blew the dust from the photo. It was one she had never seen — Kim standing next to a tanned, smiling, athletic-looking man slightly taller than herself. Both wore sky-blue puffy parkas and fuzzy hats with emblems: *Blue Angel Lodge*. Two pairs of skis stood upright in the snow beside them. Kelly's lips curved in a smile of disbelief. She would have to see it to believe it. Never in her entire life had Kim wanted to ski. Now she recalled that Kim had mentioned taking a lesson from a really super instructor.

Hmmm, thought Kelly, if Kim had found someone to dote on, someone to dote on her, Kelly couldn't be happier for her. Of the two of them, she herself had always been the effervescent, outgoing twin. Kim, shy and reserved, had seldom dated. Maybe Kim had changed. Kelly studied the picture more closely, trying to detect any changes in her sister who had chucked the New York City rat race to live in the peace and quiet of a small abandoned mining town in Colorado. Fondly she scanned the oval face framed by long, silken blonde hair; the warm, trusting brown eyes; the dimpled chin and broad smile that held a hint of mischief. She could have been looking at her own image, except that her own blonde hair was cut short, swept back from her face in the modish style she thought suited a career girl who spent all her days dealing with business people in New York.

With a feeling of satisfaction, she turned her attention to Kim's companion. There was a clean-cut, straightforward look about his features that bespoke honesty and sincerity: the sort of man a mother would trust with her daughter. Who was this good-looking athletic man her shy, introverted sister had taken up with?

She started at the sound of a vigorous pounding on the front door. She got to her feet and, glancing out the window, saw a black and white patrol car parked in the street. She opened the door to a tall, thin gangling policeman with a long solemn face, a long neck, and arms too long for his sleeves. Sweeping off his hat, he introduced himself as Officer Toomey. Once inside, his impassive gaze swept the room. He ambled to the front door and examined the lock. "No visible signs of forced entry?" Kelly shook her head. He turned and sauntered down the hall, Kelly following him into the kitchen. His gaze riveted on the note lying on the counter, the knife beside it.

Kelly blushed. "I shouldn't have touched the knife — taken down the note. I was so upset and angry that anyone would do such a thing, I didn't think —"

"It's okay, ma'am. We don't need them."

"What about fingerprints? Don't you do some lab work, some investigating?"

"Only if we've got something to go on. I expect your prints are all over the knife. Anyway, it's hard to get a clear set of prints, and if we do, most of the time we can't match 'em up to anybody."

Kelly began to feel uneasy. Officer Toomey was taking all this far too casually — in fact, he was acting like a Boy Scout who'd just stopped by to do his good deed for the day.

"Do you want to tell me what's missing, ma'am?"

Embarrassed, Kelly said, "I don't really know if anything's missing. I'm just visiting. My sister lives here."

"Where's your sister?"

"I don't know." Realizing how inane that sounded, she said, "But she ought to be home — soon."

Officer Toomey regarded her impassively. "Yes, ma'am."

"Well, what are you going to do about this — this break-in?"

Officer Toomey fixed her with an apologetic stare. "Not much we can do about it, ma'am. Actually, there's no sign of a break-in, no visible sign of forced entry, and you can't say if anything is missing —"

"But that horrible threatening note! What about that?"

A patient smile crossed his youthful face. "Actually that note doesn't threaten you with anything, ma'am. What this prob'ly is, is vandals. Happens all the time. They like to cause a little ruckus, keep the police hopping."

"But that's terrible, that people have to put up with that sort of thing!"

"Yes, ma'am, I agree. I grew up in this town and it used to be a nice quiet place where everybody knew everybody else. But times have changed. All these new ski resorts bring a lot of strangers to town — lotta young kids, or gangs looking for excitement — some of them get their kicks van-

21

dalizing houses — stealing. Actually, you got off a lot easier than most. If I were you, ma'am, I'd count myself lucky and just not worry any more about it. I'll turn in my report, but we've got a raft of them. It prob'ly won't happen again. I'd just forget it." He bid her good-bye and left.

Despite Officer Toomey's reassurances, worry invaded her mind. She set her lips in a determined line and told herself she was overreacting; she was bushed from the four-day drive from New York, and her fears were irrational. Vandalism was common. She mustn't take it as a personal attack. And of course there was some perfectly logical explanation for Kim being gone. Grimly she began setting things to rights.

She had almost finished straightening the room when the phone beside her let out a shrill ring. Kim! It must be Kim! She snatched up the receiver and answered with a warm, cheery "Hello."

A low, angry male voice said, "You have something that belongs to me. I want it back, now." His tone turned menacing. "Do you want me to come out there to get it?"

"No!" exclaimed Kelly. "And besides, you have the wrong —" Before she could explain that she wasn't Kim, the phone went dead.

An unreasoning fear seized her. Whoever the man was, he sounded so intimidating that the last thing she wanted was for him to come to Kim's chalet. If he did come, she wasn't going to be here! Heart thudding, she dived into the closet, fumbling along the rack for her coat, then remembered it was upstairs. Her frantic hands clutched Kim's loden-green jacket. Quickly she slipped it on. From the top shelf she grabbed a white fuzzy hat, yanked it well down over her ears, wound Kim's red-fringed scarf around her neck, and bolted out into the night, slamming the door after her. She glanced nervously from side to side at the chalets adjoining Kim's. Dark and deserted, they seemed to rebuff her. If she called for help, no one would hear her.

Fear spread through her like acid. She knew she didn't really believe Officer Toomey. She didn't believe that vandals took time to write menacing notes. Was someone watching the chalet right now? Waiting? She flew down the walk, flung herself inside the car, and locked the doors. She sat perfectly still, trying to catch her breath, to regain her composure. Maybe that call was a wrong number. Kim couldn't have anything that belonged to someone else, could she?

Kelly stared numbly into the darkness. Nothing stirred. No bird, no animal, no human being. The bitter cold night was deathly still and quiet. A tremor ran down her spine. She felt utterly alone, bereft. Where in the world was Kim?

Chapter Two

Driving down the dark, lonely road into town, Kelly gave herself a severe talking-to. She told herself that everyone at times has attacks of apprehension and dread, especially in strange, unexpected situations; her own ominous feelings didn't always mean Kim was in trouble. Maybe all she needed was a hot meal and a good night's sleep. But the fact remained that someone had ransacked Kim's house, turned it upside down, and was waiting for her to return. She stiffened her spine and gripped the wheel tighter against the knot that was forming in her stomach.

Distraught, she drove slowly down Main Street, past huge old elegant Victorian frame houses with gingerbread trim and signs advertising rooms to rent, to the business district she had zipped past on her way through town. Old-fashioned white-globed street lamps lined the wide street, and the frontier flavor had been retained in the original false-high-fronted store buildings, the lovely old opera house, stone-block jail, and Romanesque sandstone bank. The picturesque mining town had definitely taken a new lease on life as a ski resort. Tonight the place was buzzing with people, many of them ski bums, she thought, the weekend crowd who had just arrived and were doing their Friday shopping.

She passed the firehouse, a pharmacy, and Elliott's Hardware Company and parked before a brightly lit supermarket wedged between an antique shop and a rustic-looking restaurant, the Italian Grotto.

Inside the store she found Cleo's favorite brand of cat food, tossed a package of hamburger and a small steak into her basket along with bread, milk, orange juice, and frozen vegetables, and checked out. Bitter cold air stung her cheeks and eyelids. Calmer now, she inhaled deeply. Lasagna! Her steps slowed. Well, why not? If Kim had come home, she would have had dinner hours earlier. If Kim wasn't there, just the thought of going back to the deserted chalet, cooking a meal, and eating it alone depressed her. A hot, spicy lasagna, a tossed green salad, a chunk of crusty Italian bread, and a glass of Chianti would do wonders for her morale.

She loaded the groceries into the car and headed for the Italian Grotto. As she stepped inside she had a quick impression of beige stuccoed walls hung with posters of Venetian gondolas, Pisa's Leaning Tower, and other Italian scenes. Wrought-iron and amber-glass lanterns shed a soft golden light over tables spread with red-and-white-checked cloths. At this late hour the crowd had thinned, and the hostess led Kelly to a small table facing the door.

After a waitress took her order, Kelly sat back and forced herself to relax, enjoying the pleasant ambiance and listening to the soft, romantic mandolin music wafting through the room, apparently from no-where. The place reminded her of Rudolfo's, a favorite haunt of hers and Brad's.

Thank heaven she had escaped him! His high-powered sales pitch had become more than a person could endure. Smiling to her-self, she shook her head. No matter how many times she refused him, he persisted in his campaign to marry her. To be fair, she couldn't hold it against him. Advertising was in his blood. It was his nature, and one of the reasons his agency was so successful in New York, and the reason she had asked him to design a series of brochures to advertise her own company, Conover Executive Suites. Her new Mustang attested to his success, she thought wryly. But her interlude with Brad was past history.

When the waitress set Kelly's plate before her, she ate slowly, savoring the pasta, sipping the wine, enjoying watching the diners coming and going. Suddenly her heart gave a lurch. A tall ruddy-cheeked man with curling black hair, heavy black brows, and dark, deep-set eyes, clad in royal-blue ski togs, strode through the doorway. For one heart-stopping second, she thought he was Brad.

Strangely, perversely, she missed Brad. Sternly she reminded herself of her priorities: God, family — which meant only Kim — and career. She would make her mark in the world with a nationwide network of Executive Suites. She would allow no entangling alliance, no heartrending affair, no marriage to interfere. Brad was nice enough, but he was too intense for comfort. She wanted her own life; there was plenty of time later for marriage. Right now there were so many more ideas she wanted to see through at Executive Suites. She was fiercely independent; her freedom meant everything to her. If there was one thing she couldn't endure, it was being tied down to anyone. She had thought the Christmas holiday with Kim would be just the thing — would give her time to get used to life without Brad.

Her musing was interrupted by the sound of a high shrill voice exclaiming, "What's *she* doing here!"

Startled, Kelly glanced up, her gaze darting about the room. Her attention was caught by a petite, clear-skinned, fox-faced girl with straight, shining black hair and narrow, ice-blue eyes, standing just inside the entrance. The girl was staring straight at her, her thin lips compressed in an angry line. Their eyes met, locked, and held. Kelly's heart constricted. Never had anyone looked at her with such venom.

Abruptly the girl turned to a slender, freckle-faced female, with a crop of short, springy, carrot-red curls, who was standing at her side. In loud, disagreeable tones, she asked, "What's *she* doing back in town?"

Shrugging, her companion regarded Kelly curiously.

The dark-haired girl turned, glared at Kelly, and said loudly, "I hoped we were rid of her for good!"

Just then the hostess led them through the maze of tables and seated them across the room from Kelly. The dark-haired girl's eyes seemed drawn to her as if by a magnet. Every time Kelly glanced in her direction, the girl was staring at her with something akin to loathing. Embarrassed, Kelly blushed and looked down at her plate, her mind whirling.

Obviously, the girls had mistaken her for Kim. Her first impulse was to stride to their table, state who she was, and ask where Kim had gone. But in view of the girls' hostility, she thought better of it. Facing them down could make an unpleasant situation worse. Incredible as it seemed, Kim had made an enemy! Her kind, quiet sister! It was hard to believe, but there it was. An enemy of Kim's was an enemy of hers.

Actually the girl had done her a favor, thought Kelly wryly. Now she knew that Kim had gone away somewhere. But where? Why hadn't Kim mentioned a trip in her letters? Well, that was plain enough; she hadn't known she was going. The spoiled food in her fridge bore that out. Maybe her boss had sent her off on a short business trip. Or — maybe she had misjudged Kim. Maybe her old-fashioned, mid-Victorian sister had taken off on a holiday with a man and simply wasn't telling! The image of the tanned, athletic-looking man at Kim's side in the photo flashed into her mind. She grinned to herself. Unlikely, but possible. In any case, Kim would surely be home in time to go to work on Monday.

She began to relax. The tension began to drain from her body. When she looked up next and saw the fox-faced girl still glaring at her, she gave her a bland stare, tipped her glass in mock salute, and took a sip of Chianti. For dessert she ordered almond-flavored tortoni. By the time she finished, her customary cheerful outlook had revived.

With all the dignity she could muster, head held high, she strode from the Italian Grotto without a backward glance. Her feeling of well-being lasted all the way back to the chalet.

It wasn't until she walked through the door, greeted only by the cats howling their hunger, that she realized how much she had counted on Kim's having returned. The silent rooms seemed to echo with a hollow, empty sound, mocking her.

She fed the cats and, resolving not to dwell on the threatening note and phone call, flopped down on the couch to watch TV, but her mind refused to focus. Determined not to worry about Kim, Kelly tried not to think about her, but the harder she tried, the more she was tormented with troublesome thoughts of Kim.

31

Shortly after midnight, Kelly got up and drew back the draperies, leaving exposed a yard-wide square of black night. She turned on the small, sandstone table lamp in front of the window, in case Kim returned during the night.

Dispiritedly she climbed the stairs to the loft, undressed, and dropped onto Kim's king-size bed. Sleep eluded her. Treacherous thoughts whirled around in her head like a pinwheel in a stiff breeze. Where had Kim gone? And with whom? Where was Brad? And with whom? Not that she really cared about him! She was just curious. Deep down inside, she felt an aching emptiness that she wouldn't allow herself to analyze.

Chapter Three

It was the silence that woke her: an unearthly, deathly stillness, an alien sound totally unlike the familiar, reassuring sounds of blaring horns, screeching brakes, and sirens she was used to hearing wafting upward past the windows of her brownstone row house in Manhattan.

Momentarily disoriented, she jumped, startled by a sudden creaking sound, then laughed at herself. The heater had kicked on, blowing hot air through cold metal ducts. She glanced at the clock on the nightstand. Twenty after three. And then she heard it: a slight thump, like a door or a drawer closing. Then silence, a weird, waiting silence. Kelly's heart thudded violently. Her hands clutching the sheet grew moist. Had someone broken into the chalet? A familiar yowl echoed through the darkness. She smiled sheepishly at her foolish fears. That itchy-footed cat Cleo had jumped down from a chair in the kitchen and was howling to go out. She switched on the red pottery bedside lamp, grabbed her fleecy robe from the foot of the bed, and put it on. Halfway to the stairs she heard it again: a vague, indefinable sound of hurried movement, then a thud, like someone bumping into something in the dark. A scream rose in her throat, but no sound came out.

Suddenly aware that if the intruder looked up he would see her silhouetted against the light, Kelly dropped to the floor facedown, flattening her body against the carpet. Cautiously she peered through the railing, but she could see only a huge hulking shape in the dark living room below, hurrying toward the front door. Now she noticed he'd left it slightly ajar. The cold air had rushed in, triggering the heater whose creaking sounds had made her pause and listen. Clearly the intruder didn't want to be caught any more than she did, for the next instant he fled out the door.

Kelly leaped to her feet, ran down the stairs, slammed the door and locked it, then crossed to the desk to call the police. It was then she saw that once again the desk drawers had been rifled.

Sooner than she would have believed possible, she heard a siren screaming down the street, then a knock on the door. Kelly opened it to behold Officer Toomey standing on the threshold. Her heart sank. He was the last person she'd choose to investigate anything. Why was he here?

As if reading her thoughts, he said, "I'm on the graveyard shift this week, ma'am."

Once inside he made a thorough check of the house and found nothing. "Just a prowler, ma'am. Nothing to worry about."

Kelly bristled. "Listen, Officer Toomey, this *prowler* seems to have no trouble at all just walking in the door."

He nodded agreeably. "Prob'ly somebody who knows your sister, has a key. Looks like he thought she was out and just came in to get warm."

Annoyed, Kelly snapped, "I doubt that very much! Furthermore, I don't think the police are taking this very seriously."

The officer looked offended and indignant at the same time. "Nothing's missing, is it?"

"Not that I know of." Still she felt the man was resisting her, refusing to help. Her temper rose. "What shall I do? Should I have the locks changed or a deadbolt put on?"

"You could, ma'am. But it won't do any good. If a person really wants to get in a place, he can always find a way."

Kelly felt as though he had just tossed a bucket of ice water over her. Anxiety made her voice high and sharp. "I want the police to *do* something. I don't want this to happen again!"

"Yes, ma'am. It prob'ly won't, once your sister gets home."

"That's another thing. I'm worried about my sister! I still haven't heard a word from her."

"You worry too much, ma'am. She'll come back when she's ready." Officer Toomey managed a grin. "Meanwhile, I'll let you know if we catch any prowlers. Then you can rest easy."

The last thing she'd do would be to rest easy, thought Kelly, showing him out the door. It wasn't until after she was in bed that she began to puzzle over what made Officer Toomey think all her troubles would end when Kim came home. But she was more tired than she realized. Sleep overtook her before she could think it through.

Morning came all too soon. Kelly glanced at the empty space beside her and felt a swift stab of disappointment. If Kim had slipped inside the chalet in the small dark hours of the night, she'd be there, stretched out flat on her stomach; head resting on one arm; long, silken hair tumbling about her shoulders. Hoping against hope, Kelly slid from the bed and ran to the railing to peer down over the living room. No slender figure was curled up in a chair, or stretched out on the couch. The sandstone table lamp before the window sent out a feeble glow.

A sudden movement caught her eye. Through the picture window in the opening between the draperies, she glimpsed swirling flakes drifting down. Shivering, she turned away. A feeling of foreboding, like the shadow of a buzzard's wings hovering overhead, swept through her. She mustn't give in to it, must pull herself together. What she needed was a hot cup of coffee. She slipped into a long white woolly robe and went downstairs.

She felt slightly cheered when she opened the kitchen door and the cats rushed to greet her, rubbing their warm bodies against her legs. By the time she finished feeding the cats, the coffee had brewed, and she sat down at Kim's kitchen table with her mug while her mind whirled in circles.

It was foolish to worry about Kim, she told herself firmly. With desperate urgency, she ticked off all the reasons Kim might be away. For instance, she could have gone to

Denver for the weekend, shopping for new clothes to impress her skiing friend. The small voice inside her head said, *That's what I would do, not Kim.* Or she could have lost a contact lens, and gone to Denver for a new one. *Kim does not lose things,* argued the small voice. Well, then, maybe she'd grown bored with Blue Angel, and hungry for big-city life, and took off on a holiday.

The cats finished eating and clustered around the kitchen door. She got up, let them out, and stood watching them wade through the snow, lifting each foot high. Though it had stopped snowing, they scampered quickly back to the door, mewling to come inside.

Kelly let them in, poured herself another cup of coffee, and sank down in a kitchen chair. A holiday in Denver was at least possible, she conceded. After all, Kim had grown up in the city. It was her natural habitat. When they had started Conover Executive Suites almost a year ago, working out of their New York brownstone, it was what both of them wanted. Bursting with enthusiasm, their heads full of plans, they agreed they'd make a terrific team. Kelly had leased office space uptown and rounded up clients who needed temporary office space and part-time secretarial services. Kim had kept the accounts.

How Kim loved to keep the books, thought Kelly, smiling reflectively. Neat and orderly by nature, she loved to set records straight. In fact, it was Kim who, six months ago, announced in flat, unequivocal tones that their business couldn't support the two of them. Almost apologetically she said, "And if you want the whole truth, I detest living in New York City!" At Kelly's look of astonishment, she grinned and said, "Are you ready for this? What I'm dying to do is defect, move to Blue Angel where there's a little peace and quiet, and dig up our family tree. And since we're the only ones left, and we have only an old land grant and the names in the family Bible to go on, it would be a real challenge."

When Kelly started to protest, Kim waved a sheet of figures under her nose. "Just look at this profit and loss statement! We're barely making ends meet. Now's the time, Kelly — when Executive Suites is struggling to get on its feet — the ideal time for me to give it a go. When I finish tracking down the Conovers in Colorado, and the business *really* needs me, I'll fly back."

At first Kelly had argued with her, swore she'd eat beans every night, if that's all they could afford, so long as Kim didn't leave. But Kim was adamant, as stubborn as Kelly herself.

Gradually it came to Kelly that Kim wanted to leave for another reason, one she wasn't telling. Whether Kim was unaware of it, or whether she kept silent for fear of hurting Kelly's feelings, Kelly had no way of knowing. All she understood was that Kim had to leave, to become her own person. Kelly's heart gave a painful twist. Had she hogged the limelight, putting Kim in the shadows all their lives? Or had Kim felt she'd used Kelly as a crutch, and now had to prove herself? Giving way, she saw Kim off with a misty-eyed hug, a kiss, and her blessing.

To Kelly's surprise, it was she herself, the extrovert, the twin with the stronger personality of the two, who felt as though she'd lost an arm and a leg. At first she thought Kim would feel the same way, and waited with cheerful optimism for a letter bearing the news of Kim's return to New York.

Kim's letters came, exuding happy enthusiasm. Mr. Clark Teague, owner of the Alpenstock Land Development Corporation, had hired her to run his office. Business was slow. Mr. Teague and his salesman were gone much of the time, leaving Kim plenty of free time to track down their Conover ancestors. Kelly, in an effort to boost her spirits, had gone skiing in Vermont, and Brad York had come into her life. Nobody could be lonely with Brad around.

Yes, it was possible that Kim could miss the bright lights, the excitement of New York, but it wasn't probable. Her letters, rather than betraying boredom and discontent, were happy and carefree. In any case, Kim would be home by Sunday night to go to work on Monday morning. There was no earthly reason why she should be home before then.

And there was nothing more she herself could do now. Always, in the past, taking to the slopes had given her a new perspective. Maybe skiing down the Blue Angel trails would clear her mind, help her think through the events of the last two days, give her some inspiration as to the why, when, and where Kim had gone.

Half an hour later, Kelly, clad in a pink parka and ski pants, was seated behind the wheel of her car tooling toward the ski area, leaving a tightly locked condo behind. The narrow graveled road wound through a broad, snow-covered valley rimmed by the cathedral peaks of Blue Angel Mountain. Gazing at the long sloping folds, like white ermine robes strewn with blue-green firs, she recalled Kim telling her that the stands of blue spruce spread over the snowy slopes of the highest peak flanked by curved, winglike crests, had inspired the name Blue Angel.

She turned her attention to the winding road, keeping an eye cocked for the small blue and white signposts pointing the way toward Blue Angel Lodge. As she drew near, her uneasy mood gave way to excitement and anticipation at the prospect of conquering new, challenging runs. Rounding a curve, she saw a line of blue chair lifts climbing up the side of the nearest peak.

Though it was early in the season, the runs were mobbed. Soon Kelly was waiting her turn in the lift line, chatting with other skiers. At length she zipped up from the valley to an altitude of nearly eleven thousand feet. Sliding off the chair lift, she glided down the ramp toward Hell's Fire run, whose black signpost marked it as an advanced trail for expert skiers. Moments later, she dug her poles in and pushed off.

Under a deep blue sky, warm sun, and clear, bracing air, Kelly felt as though she were floating down through the forest. As she skied, shafts of sunlight streaming through the trees, all her problems fell away:

her anxiety over Kim; her perverse, inexplicable feeling of missing Brad; her continuing crises juggling employees and equipment. Soaring down the vast, bright, white-powdered slope, she couldn't imagine any greater joy than just being alive in this place, on this day.

Speeding down the tree-studded run, Kelly heard a sudden shout behind her. Her head whipped around. Two skiers were gaining on her, two men, one clad in bright green, the other a tall reedy man in dark blue ski togs wearing yellow-tinted sunglasses. The man in blue waved a hand in salute, but as they flew past her Kelly saw a startled expression come over his face. His eyes hardened into a glare. On the face of his companion she saw a puzzled look swiftly replaced by an affronted expression, as if he were insulted by her blank, unresponsive gaze. Before she could raise a hand to wave back, they were barreling down the run.

Apparently they had mistaken her for Kim. No doubt the reedy skier was surprised, and clearly disapproved of Kim, a novice, trying an advanced slope. And his friend probably wondered why she hadn't recognized him. As she crested a short rise, she saw them far below her, nearing the end of the run. Deliberately she swerved right, veering toward a longer, gentler slope so she'd be sure to avoid meeting them at the bottom. Who needs more hostility? she thought grimly.

After a morning of skiing, Kelly's knees felt tired, her legs ached, her heart pounded in her chest. Breathless and exhausted, she trudged inside Alpen Haus, a cafeteria midway up the mountain. She gulped a cup of hot chocolate and a mushroom quiche, then hurried back to the lift to explore another run. An orange ball of fire was dipping over the distant rocky summits as she caught the last chair lift to the top of Rainbow Run and made a final descent over knee-deep powder that ended in a breathtaking drop-off.

Dusk had fallen by the time Kelly turned down the dirt road to Alpine Village and pulled up before number twelve. No light shone from the darkened chalet, and only the cats bounded out to greet her, waving their tails in welcome. Usually she shut them in the kitchen. Now she was glad she'd forgotten.

Disheartened, she moved mechanically about the kitchen. Like a dog worrying a bone, her mind fastened on Kim. After dinner she told herself sharply, "You're not going to spend another evening brooding over Kim!" She got up, marched into the living room, and scanned the bookshelves for something to read.

Her gaze swept past the family Bible, paused, then swept back again. The padded brown leather cover was a work of art, thought Kelly admiringly, with finely drawn biblical scenes etched in gold, and the book itself must be all of five inches thick. Curiously she leafed through the gilt-edged pages interspersed with black and white etchings and full-color illustrations.

Halfway through the book, she came to a thick page beautifully illuminated with a church bell, a golden ring, white blossoms, and doves. Softly she read: "This certifies that Walter F. Conover and Nellie R. Hill were joined together by me in the Bonds of Holy Matrimony at Blue Angel on the eighteenth day of April in the year of our Lord 1887, in the presence of Mr. Horace Hall and Mrs. Horace Hall. Signed, John Dalton Williams." Great-grandmother and great-grandfather, thought Kelly wistfully.

Intrigued, she carried the heavy Bible to the kitchen table and sat down. Eagerly she turned the pages. After the certificate of holy matrimony was a page of family marriages, followed by two pages of births and deaths. Slowly, carefully, she perused the dates and names. There she saw inscribed, in bright blue ink: "September 28, 1959, Kelly and Kim Conover." A strange feeling stole over her. These were her people. Had it not been for them, she and Kim would never have existed. In a sudden burst of understanding, she sympathized with Kim's compulsion to trace the beginnings of their family.

Head bent, chin propped on her hands, Kelly browsed through the book. At last she closed the brown padded cover and sat up straight, her mind seething with questions. Who had settled in Blue Angel before her great-grandparents? What had become of them? What had Kim learned about them?

Impulsively she went to Kim's built-in desk in the living room. In one of her letters, Kim had mentioned that she was making progress "unearthing" family skeletons, but in recent months Alpenstock's sales had picked up and her search had lagged. She'd promised to send Kelly a full report when she finished, so her notes must be here somewhere.

She searched through the drawers and found nothing pertaining to the Conover genealogy. Her fine pale brows drew together in a frown. Where were Kim's notes? They were probably in her desk at work. At least there was one thing she knew for certain: Kim had started her search for Conover history at the graveyard. If she could follow in Kim's footsteps, she might find Kim. Instantly she pushed down the thought, aghast at her disquieting turn of mind. Of course she wouldn't find Kim in the graveyard. Would she?

The next morning she fished out a map of "historic" Blue Angel from the lower desk drawer, and saw that the cemetery was off county Route 8 and that she could circle past it on her way to the slopes.

"Enough of this hanging around," she told herself sternly. Within half an hour she was on her way.

She guided the car along the winding county road past a snowy meadow, curving around a lake whose waters mirrored a forest of dark spruce and a Delft-blue sky. At length she saw a sign pointing the way to Blue Angel Cemetery. She swung right, then doubled back and followed a dirt road to the graveyard, set among a grove of aspen and evergreens.

In the hushed stillness she walked slowly toward the graves marked with carved stones, some still standing upright, some fallen. Several were enclosed by rusted iron fences — to keep out the wild animals, thought Kelly, shuddering. She paused to read the epitaphs carved on the granite markers. Many bore the names of entire families wiped out in epidemics, or babies who had died before their first birthdays.

She stopped short before a tall, arched headstone decorated with angels and vines. The crescent-carved name seemed to leap out at her. CONOVER. Beneath the surname, she could just make out: Walter E. Born October 3, 1857. Died August 12, 1924. An odd feeling of unreality came over her. Here lay her great-grandfather.

She turned toward the next grave. It, too, bore the name Conover. It was a low, rounded stone with a cherubic-looking baby's head chiseled at the top. She read aloud: "Luke Conover, son of W. and N. R. Conover. Died May 6, 1889, aged 6 months, 27 days. Gone but not forgotten."

Kelly swallowed hard and moved on. It was then she heard it: a slight scuffling noise behind her, like someone shuffling through snow-crusted leaves. She whirled around, letting out a shriek that seemed to rise to the treetops and then dissipate into the vast blue sky. Someone was following her, hiding behind the thick green firs. She wanted to run, but her legs refused to move. She stood staring, jaw clenched. The scuffling sound came again. Kelly's head spun in the direction of the sound. She uttered an astonished cry, then felt utterly foolish. A thin gray squirrel scurried across the frozen ground and disappeared into the grove of spruce. You fool, she berated herself. This waiting game until Kim's return was making her a nervous wreck.

She moved on to an overgrown, weed-filled plot beside three leafless aspen, bordered by a low, crumbling brick wall. Time and weather had almost obliterated the carving on the face of the tall, stone obelisk. Kelly hunkered down before it and ran her fingertips over the indentations in an effort to decipher the words. At last she managed to make out: "REIMER, F. Joel. Born May 22, 1853. Died February 5, 1873. F. Joel was lost in a snowstorm while visiting his mine on February 5, 1873, and was found June 15, 1873." Mingled horror and compassion flowed through her. Death stalked these people every day of their lives.

Feeling discouraged and depressed, she strode back to the car, thinking, I hope Kim gleaned something from those tombstones, because I certainly haven't!

She had spent more time browsing through the cemetery than she'd thought, for when she drove through town, church-goers were sauntering out the doorway of the white clapboard Presbyterian church. The sight of them triggered an idea. Churches kept records! A church could be a gold mine of information. Her own parents had been Lutheran. At a stoplight she glanced at the map. Faith Lutheran Church was on Main Street, past the post office and jail in the block before the old Antlers Hotel. She drove on.

Faith Lutheran was a square, red brick building with tall, round-arched windows and an imposing bell tower. Apparently the pastor had a long message, thought Kelly wryly, for Faith Lutheran had not let out. The wide street, crowded with Sunday strollers, was lined with cars, and there was no place to park. She drove past Gilpin Street, past the Antlers Hotel, and found a space a block away.

She walked swiftly back toward the church along the brick-paved sidewalk, threading her way through throngs of people. Passing the hotel, she noticed two men, garbed in dark topcoats and Stetson hats, standing on the steps talking animatedly. The shorter of the two, a beefy, red-faced man, waved an arm through the air, as if to emphasize his words. Kelly's at-

50

tention was caught by a diamond ring flashing on one of his thick, stubby fingers.

His gaze locked with hers. His mouth fell open in a double-take. In a split second she read shock, astonishment, and recognition in his half-lidded, stony gray eyes. No smile lighted his heavy features. He seemed to bristle with hostility. Kelly walked faster, watching him from the corner of her eye. Abruptly he bolted down the steps to the sidewalk, shoving people out of his way, striding toward her.

He gripped her arm roughly, jerking her to a halt. An angry flush suffused his face. In hard, sharp tones he snapped, "Not so fast, lady. You're coming with me. We're going to have a little talk — in private."

An unreasoning fear seized her. What was the matter with the people in this town? With a quick twist of her arm, she wrenched free of his grasp and lunged away from the man, running headlong down the street, bumping into people in her effort to elude him. Heedless of an oncoming jeep, she darted across Gilpin Street, dashing down Main. The crowd thickened. Faith Lutheran's congregation was spilling out of the church in a welcome tide. A peal of bells from the steeple seemed to clang in her ears, as if sounding a warning.

Kelly barged into the midst of the crowd, mingling with people who had paused to chat, weaving her way up the steps. She slipped around two white-haired ladies chatting with the pastor and darted through the door. Once inside, she glanced frantically around the narthex. Seeing no place to hide, she dashed into the sanctuary, squeezing past people filing out the center aisle. There, in one of the straight wooden pews, she sank down gasping for breath, praying the menacing-looking stranger wouldn't follow her.

She closed her eyes and took a deep breath to compose herself. Enough was enough! The jet-haired, fox-faced girl at the Italian Grotto had stared at her spitefully, the tall reedy skier on the slope had been clearly hostile, and now this lummox had not only glared at her vengefully but had hulked after her with blood in his eye. She could no longer brush off what would be obvious to a ten-year-old child: Kim had made enemies in this town. A tremor of mingled apprehension and fear ran down her spine. What on earth could Kim have done? And where on earth was she? No matter how hard Kelly tried, she could no longer convince herself that her fears were irrational and groundless. They were all too frighteningly real.

Chapter Four

Sitting there in the quiet church, Kelly quickly surveyed the white walls, the high vaulted ceiling, and the tide of people rising from their seats, strolling from the sanctuary. Above the altar, shafts of jewel-toned light streamed through a stained-glass window. She closed her eyes and took a deep breath. The murmur of warm, friendly voices flowed past her as the last of the congregation moved slowly down the red-carpeted aisle. Suddenly she sensed someone standing beside her, hovering over her at the end of the wooden pew. She stiffened, hardly daring to breathe. Had the man followed her all the way inside the church?

"Are you all right?" The voice was soft and deep, with only a trace of a German accent.

Her eyes flew open. At her side stood a short, rotund man clad in a black robe and long white surplice. His sparse gray hair was combed to one side, and bright, penetrating blue eyes peered through gold-rimmed spectacles. A look of gentle concern shone from his round, kindly face.

"I'm Pastor Meyer. You're welcome to sit here as long as you like. Or, if there's some problem you'd care to discuss . . ."

Kelly glanced furtively over her shoulder. Her eyes widened. Shoving through the doorway, bucking the departing crowd, was her grim-faced pursuer, his stony eyes alight with anger. Close to panic, she jumped up from the pew and faced Pastor Meyer, her lips curved in a quick smile of mingled relief and hope. "Yes, you can help me!" she said eagerly. "But I'd much rather discuss the matter in your office."

The pastor nodded and escorted her down the aisle toward a door to the left of the altar. Walking close to his side, Kelly explained that she and her sister were trying to trace the Conover family.

Pastor Meyer nodded, smiling understandingly. "We've had many such requests. I'll be glad to show you our records."

She darted another quick look over her shoulder and saw her beefy adversary poised just inside the doorway, fists clenched at his sides, glaring at her, clearly furious at being thwarted in his attempt to catch her. What's going on here? she wondered. If the man were on the up-and-up, he'd have no hesitation in confronting her here and now, under the pastor's protective eye.

Pastor Meyer ushered her through the door into a small office redolent with the spicy aroma of pipe tobacco, and motioned her toward a green leather chair beside an ancient desk, swept clean except for a brass rack full of letters and a pipe stand full of pipes. From a shelf on a wall, he took down three black leather-bound volumes and set them on the desk.

"Here we are," he said affably. *"Marriages, Births,* and *Deaths."* Easing his short, bulky frame onto a chair, he pulled the top book from the stack and flipped it open.

"Let's see — Conover . . ." With a practiced finger he ran quickly down the column of names.

Kelly leaned forward, her eyes following his finger down the page. "I'll be glad to search through the books if there's something else you need to do."

"No, no, it's quite all right."

Kelly stifled a sigh. It was going to take forever to go through all three books.

As if sensing her impatience, Pastor Meyer pushed the book labeled *Deaths* toward her. "You can browse through this one, if you like."

An ironic grin twisted the corners of her mouth. Could anyone *like* to browse through *Deaths*?

She pulled her chair closer to the desk and opened the book.

"Ah! Here we are," said Pastor Meyer with a jubilant grin. "Robert Milton Conover, born September 9, 1905, to Walter and Nellie Conover."

Kelly felt a quick thrill of elation. "Robert was my grandfather; Walter and Nellie were my great-grandparents. There should be a record of my father's birth, in 1938."

Pastor Meyer took up the volume of births and paged through it. "Yes, here it is: John Conover, born March 14, 1938, to Robert and Elizabeth Conover." He continued flipping through the pages.

Kelly looked down at the first page of deaths, then glanced back at Pastor Meyer. "This book begins with 1900. My sister and I want to know about our ancestors in the 1800s — when our family first came to Blue Angel. Have you another book . . . ?"

Pastor Meyer gave a helpless shrug. "I'm sure we *had* others, but the original structure housing Faith Lutheran was a wooden building erected in 1869. In November of

1897 it went up in flames — burned to the ground. All of our records were lost."

Kelly felt as though the wind had been knocked out of her. "Nothing! No records at all?"

Regretfully Pastor Meyer shook his head. "None. I'm sorry." He rose from his chair and crossed to a filing cabinet in the corner. "There is one other bit of information I may be able to give you." He pulled open a drawer, leafed through a dog-eared folder, and withdrew a form. Cheerfully he said, "Our records show that on August 17, 1935, a letter of transfer was granted to Robert and Elizabeth Conover to Trinity Lutheran Church."

Kelly nodded. "That could be very helpful. We knew our grandparents had left their farm in the valley, but we weren't certain when."

"Now you know, my dear. In 1935." Pastor Meyer sighed heavily. "From 1932 through 1937 were years of prolonged droughts and high winds. They caused great damage through soil erosion in eastern and southeastern Colorado. It was impossible to scratch a living from the land. It was the Great Depression and many people left." Suddenly his face broke into a grin. "Apparently your grandfather took off for greener pastures."

Smiling at his attempt at humor, Kelly stood up. "Thanks for the information, Pastor Meyer."

"Not much help with your ancestors, I'm afraid." As he walked with her to his office door a twinkle came into his blue eyes. "Perhaps you'll visit me again, next Sunday morning at eleven."

An answering sparkle lit Kelly's eyes. "I'll do my best."

She stood in the doorway of the church, squinting in the bright sunlight. The congregation had thinned by now, gone for lunch or an afternoon of skiing, she imagined. Cautiously she stepped through the doorway and stood poised at the top of the white stone steps. Looking up and down the street, she tried to scan every doorway. There was no sign of her hefty, grim-eyed pursuer. He must have lost the chase in the crowd of churchgoers. Relief flowed through her.

With determined cheer, she promised herself she would ski till dark. She'd take home a pizza for supper, build a roaring fire in the great stone fireplace, read or watch TV, and wait up for Kim. In the morning when she awoke, Kim would be home.

When Kelly awoke on Monday morning, Kim was not home. All her fears and apprehensions returned. Desperately she went over in her mind all the reasons why Kim would be gone, but they no longer reassured her. Sick with worry, she told herself over and over again that Kim could take care of herself. It made no difference. She was through with making assumptions and rationalizations. She had to know where Kim was, and she had to know now.

She dressed hastily, pulling on a red-and-white-striped sweater and navy blue slacks. She fed the cats and fixed breakfast for herself. Impatiently she watched the green digits on Kim's microwave clock till they flicked to 9:00. It was time to go.

After pulling on her boots, she donned Kim's green jacket and knitted ski cap and let herself out the front door. Purposefully she strode to the first chalet in the row and rang the bell. No one answered. Undaunted, she continued down the deserted street, ringing bells, knocking on doors, passing by chalets with **FOR SALE** signs stuck in the frozen ground.

No one seemed to be home. She back-tracked past Kim's house and strode to the door of number fourteen. Figured draperies covered the picture window, and an iron pot filled with dead ice-encrusted plants stood by the front door. No one answered her knock. She strode briskly on. There were cars parked in front of only two of the chalets: a red VW at the end of the row, and a shiny black Cadillac before number sixteen. This should have told her something, thought Kelly dismally. But the people who lived here could have taken off early to ski.

She came abreast of the Cadillac and strode up the walk. Inside a TV was blasting and her hopes soared. A sleepy-eyed blonde woman wearing a flowered robe, her hair in pink foam rollers, answered her knock. She glanced at Kelly with mildly inquisitive eyes. The thought flashed through Kelly's mind that the woman showed no sign of recognition. At least *she* isn't mistaking me for Kim, thought Kelly, feeling relieved and uneasy at the same time.

"I'm Kelly Conover — visiting my sister in number twelve. She didn't expect me here till the twenty-third and she isn't home. I wonder if you know where she is?"

"Sorry, I wouldn't know." The woman sounded miffed, almost resentful, as if Kelly had asked for her bank balance.

"Do you remember when you last saw her?"

"I dunno. What's she look like?"

Kelly grinned. "She looks exactly like me. We're twins."

The woman cocked her head, eyeing Kelly thoughtfully. "Yeah, I think I did see a girl that looks like you, going out with some man. Must have been a week or so ago."

"What did the man look like?"

The woman shrugged. "It was almost dark, and I wasn't paying attention. I don't spy on my neighbors."

"What about the car? What make car was he driving?"

Again the woman shrugged. "Sorry, I can't tell one car from another. They all look the same to me."

"I see. Thanks anyway."

"No bother." The door closed quickly.

Kelly turned away, disappointment knifing through her. She hurried past two more vacant chalets to the last one on the block, where the VW was parked. At her knock, the door slowly swung open, but she saw no one.

"Yes?" said a small voice.

She glanced down. A tiny, pajama-clad, curly-haired boy, about three years old, she guessed, peered at her from behind the door.

"Hello, I'm your neighbor in number twelve. Is your mother home?"

"No."

"Is your father home?"

"He's skiing with my mother. My brother and sister aren't here either. They're skiing with Mom and Dad."

With an effort, Kelly put down her impatience. "Are you here alone?"

The boy grinned. "No. Helen's here."

"Will you ask Helen to come to the door, please?"

The boy turned his head and yelled, "Helen, come here!"

A shaggy white sheepdog with black ears lumbered to the door and sniffed interestedly at Kelly's boots.

The boy grinned. "Helen's my dog. My meemaw's here, too."

"Your meemaw?" asked Kelly uncertainly.

A pleasant-looking gray-haired woman in her sixties emerged from the kitchen, wiping her hands on a towel. "Who is it, Robbie?"

"I don't know, Meemaw. Some lady wants to see Mom."

The woman came to the door. Kelly introduced herself, and before she could ask if she'd seen Kim, the woman motioned her inside and closed the door.

"I'm Robbie's grandmother. My daughter won't be back till dinnertime."

Without giving Kelly a chance to speak, she rattled on, shaking her head. "This is such a lonely place, way out here in the boonies. There's nobody to talk to. A person would have a hard time even to borrow a cup of sugar!" She sniffed, then drew a tissue from her apron pocket and blew her nose delicately. "I'm afraid I've taken cold. Only five of these places are sold, you know, all the rest are empty. And some of those are just let out to people who come to ski."

Quickly Kelly broke in. "My sister rents number twelve. But she's gone off somewhere and I'm trying to find her . . ."

The woman nodded. "Oh, I've seen you in your green jacket, flying in and out number twelve. Robbie and I go for a walk every day, keep tabs on who comes and goes." She gave a friendly chuckle. "I'm looking to find me another grandma to talk to." Frowning, she took another tissue from her pocket and blew her nose. "Funny, I've never seen your sis—"

Kelly interrupted. "It was my sister you saw flying in and out."

"I saw she just got a brand-new white convertible. She won't want a convertible around here — too cold."

"That's my convertible," interrupted Kelly, trying to control her impatience. "The girl you saw at number twelve — before I came in the convertible — was my sister Kim. We're identical twins."

"Twins! Well, I never! You sure do look alike."

"Right!"

"Well, I'm sorry my daughter isn't here. She's gone skiing with —"

Kelly quickly broke in. "I'm really looking for my sister. Do you remember the last time you saw her?"

Meemaw scowled at a crack in the ceiling. "Well, let me see, it must have been a week ago, right before the last big snow — and then I saw her again getting out of your car — yesterday, I think it was."

"You saw *me* getting out of the car," said Kelly, thinking she would scream if she didn't soon get through to this likable, lonely woman. "We're identical twins . . ."

"You know, I knew some twins once, years ago, when I was in second grade, or maybe it was third grade. Even their own mama couldn't tell who was who. Every morning she'd tie different colored ribbons on their hair so she could tell 'em apart. Could your mama tell you apart?"

Kelly laughed. "Sure. I was the noisy one. Kim was quiet, and we never dressed alike. Our mother detested carbon copies. She wanted each of us to be an original." Kelly moved to the door and grasped the knob.

"Then you haven't seen my sister since last week, right?"

"I guess not, not since the last snow, because Robbie and I couldn't take our walk the next day. I'm afraid that's when I took this cold . . ."

Kelly flashed her a warm smile. "I understand. Thanks for your help." She whipped open the door and fled into the dismal gray morning.

She glanced at her watch. Almost ten. Instead of going back inside the chalet, she pulled out her keys, slid inside her car, and turned on the engine. Within half an hour she was rolling down Main Street, scanning every building for the storefront office of Kim's employer. It must be here somewhere, she thought anxiously.

She found the Alpenstock Land Development Corporation sandwiched between the First National Bank and a deli. All she could see through the window were two metal chairs and a bedraggled potted palm struggling to live. She parked the car and went inside. When Kim had said it was a small office, she hadn't been exaggerating. The walls of the long narrow room were decorated with photos of vast mountain vistas of Colorado, photos of condominiums, floor plans, and land plats. Three desks were lined up against the left wall, deserted except for the first one, which held a neat plastic nameplate reading **CINDY LAMB**. Seated behind it was a gaminlike girl with big eyes, no makeup, and wispy brown hair screwed into a knot atop her head. She wore jeans and a red tee-shirt, and around her neck was a thin gold chain from which hung a golden nugget. She looked all of eighteen. Crouching over an ancient manual typewriter, she was typing at a snail's pace. No sign of Kim, thought Kelly, taken aback. She had hoped that maybe Kim had returned and gone directly to work. Maybe she was in the washroom, though, or else on a coffee break . . .

Kelly mustered a smile and crossed to the desk. Without preamble, she said, "May I see Kim Conover, please."

The girl stopped typing and looked up. "Who?"

"Kim Conover. She works here — keeps the books . . ."

A baffled expression came over the girl's face. With nervous fingers she slid the golden nugget back and forth on the chain. "I'm the only girl who works here, and I don't know any Kim Conover."

Something like fear tugged at Kelly's heart. "How long have you worked for Alpenstock Land Development?"

"I started a week ago. Mr. Teague hired me from Temporary Help in Denver. Paid my way out here and . . ."

"Denver!"

A look of pride glistened in the girl's big brown eyes. "He said there wasn't anyone in Blue Angel smart enough to handle the job. Besides, he needed someone right away. The last girl left without a word to anybody. Just didn't come in one morning."

The fear inside Kelly spread, tightening her chest. "When was that? When was the last day she was here?"

The girl's thin brows lifted. A vague expression clouded her eyes. "Who knows?"

Kelly took a deep breath. "Maybe Mr. Teague knows. May I speak to him, please?"

"Mr. Teague is away on a business trip."

"When will he be back?" asked Kelly. It was like pulling teeth to get information from Cindy Lamb.

The girl bent over the typewriter and resumed typing. "He didn't say."

Kelly leaned over the desk, flattening her hands on the top. "Listen, Cindy." Her tone was sharp and demanding. "I have to find my sister. I have to know what day she left, if she told anyone good-bye — who saw her last."

Cindy drew back, as if fearing Kelly would leap over the desk and grab her by the throat. In a panicky voice she said, "I've told you all I know. The only other person who might have seen her is Mr. Teague's salesman — Bill Smythe."

"Where can I find him?"

Cindy shrugged. "Monday is his day off. He might be here tomorrow. He's in and out of the office a lot. I'll tell him to call you."

Kelly picked up a notepad and pencil, jotted down her phone number, and handed it to Cindy. "Now, how does he spell his name?"

"S-M-Y-T-H-E. Like *scythe,* that you cut hay with."

"Thanks." Kelly wrote it down and tucked the paper in her pocket. As she turned to leave, the girl gave her a tentative smile, clearly relieved that Kelly was finally going, leaving her unharmed.

Feeling more frustrated than ever, Kelly puzzled over why Mr. Teague had to hire help from Denver — but then, after all, he'd hired Kim from New York. Maybe he had a thing against skiers — thought they'd take to the slopes and leave him in the lurch.

One thing she did know. She wasn't going to stand around cooling her heels waiting for Teague or his salesman Smythe to show up, and she had done waiting for Kim. Stepping out of the doorway into the brilliant sunlight, she strode briskly along the brick-paved sidewalk toward the police station.

Shortly she saw what she was looking for, looming like a fortress halfway down the next block. The square two-story brick structure with iron-barred windows and arched double glass doors looked to have been built around the turn of the century. As she entered the building, doubt invaded her mind. Resolutely she put it down. She would rely on the police, her last resort — this time they would have to help her. But when she confronted the uniformed officer seated behind the main desk, she suddenly felt painfully alone and vulnerable. She thought fleetingly of Brad; it would have been nice to have him here beside her, but he was long gone. Regaining her confidence, she looked the officer squarely in the eyes and said, "I want to report a missing person."

Chapter Five

"You what?"

Kelly met Captain Creel's gaze head-on, staring directly into his shiny, jet-black eyes. He was short and slender, with ginger-colored hair and a bright, cocky air that reminded her of a roadrunner sprinting along the roadside ferreting out unwary insects.

"I want to report a missing person," repeated Kelly firmly.

Not unkindly, he said, "Have you alerted the ski patrol?"

"No, I haven't alerted the ski patrol, because I have no reason to believe the person was skiing."

A second officer shambled over to the cluttered desk and stood with his fists planted on his hips, looking curiously at Kelly. He was a chunky man in his twenties, with black hair slicked straight back, clear gray eyes, and the beginnings of a moustache, which Kelly suspected was being grown for the purpose of making him look

70

older. An appraising gleam came into his eyes.

"I'm Sergeant Gilmer. Who's missing?"

"My sister, my *twin* sister, Kim Conover."

Sergeant Gilmer's dark brows lifted. "Conover — Conover!" He snapped his fingers as if in sudden recognition and turned toward Captain Creel. "She's the little gal with the big imagination out at Alpine Village. Two calls this week — one break-in, one prowler."

An angry flush stained Kelly's cheeks. "I didn't imagine the break-in, or the prowler, and I'm certainly not imagining that my sister's missing!"

In a casual tone that did nothing to reassure Kelly of his efficiency, he asked, "Well, now, little lady, when was the last time you saw your sister?"

"Six months ago, when she left New York," said Kelly evenly. "She arrived here on June 22."

Captain Creel cleared his throat. In reproving tones he said, "People don't usually wait six months to report someone missing."

"She hasn't been *missing* for six months," said Kelly, eyeing him coldly.

In a voice tinged with irony, the captain

said, "Would you care to tell us how long she *has* been missing?"

Feeling like a dunce, Kelly said, "I'm not sure." At the officers' startled expressions, she rushed on. "But I'm sure it's been at least a week, maybe a week and a half. You see, the front walk hasn't been shoveled, and the furniture's dusty, and the food in the fridge is spoiled, and —"

Sergeant Gilmer grinned. "Sounds like my place. What's your street address again?"

Kelly tried to keep the exasperation from her voice as she gave him her name, address, and phone number. "Now may I file a missing person's report?"

Captain Creel sighed and gazed up at her, an unyielding expression of officialdom hardening his features. "I'm sorry, Miss Conover, but you have no proof whatever that your sister is actually missing. We don't file a report until the subject has been missing twenty-four hours."

Kelly felt her temper rise. She closed her eyes and took a deep breath. "I told you. I *know* she's missing because of the way she left her chalet. My sister's a demon house-keeper. She would never leave the place like that, and besides, she'd have told me if she was planning to be gone —"

Sergeant Gilmer broke in. "Listen, honey, *gone* is not *missing*. Does your sister ski?"

"No!" said Kelly, more sharply than she intended. "I mean, she's only just started taking lessons."

Captain Creel nodded, a maddening look of comprehension on his lean, angular face. As if he were reassuring a frightened child, he added, "She's probably hooked. Probably off skiing at one of the other areas with her boyfriend."

"I doubt that," snapped Kelly. "And she doesn't have a *boyfriend*."

Sergeant Gilmer chuckled. His appreciative gaze swept Kelly from head to heels. "If she looks anything like you, she *has* a boyfriend."

Kelly felt a warm flush suffuse her face. "If my sister were off skiing, she wouldn't be gone for a week and a half," insisted Kelly in agitated tones. "She has a job! She's a responsible person. She wouldn't take off without a word to anybody!" She did her best to hold back the tears forming in her eyes. "She's just *gone!*"

Sergeant Gilmer shot Captain Creel a knowing wink. He put an arm around Kelly's shoulders. His tone was warm and sympathetic. "Listen, Miss Conover, like I said, you've got to believe, 'gone' doesn't necessarily mean 'missing.' "

Kelly slid out from under his consoling arm, and saw a superior, smiling glance flash between the two men.

"Miss Conover," said the captain in dry tones, "sometimes people who don't ski *say* they're skiing when they're not. Know what I mean? They just want a little time alone."

"Yeah," agreed Sergeant Gilmer enthusiastically, "without big sister looking over their shoulder. She'll probably turn up any minute, happy as a clam."

"That often happens," said Captain Creel. "If we chased down everybody someone thought was missing, we'd have no time to deal with serious crimes."

"This *is* serious!" cried Kelly, close to tears. "Why won't you believe me? I know my sister and I know she's in trouble or she'd be here. Why won't you help me find her!"

Captain Creel got to his feet. "If your sister's missing, we'll find her, Miss Conover. If she doesn't show up within twenty-four hours, you get yourself back here, and we'll be glad to file a report." He came around the desk and clasped her elbow. Before she could protest further, he escorted her out the door.

Indignation, anger, and anxiety surged

through her. She had thought the police would help, would at least ask their patrolmen to keep an eye out for Kim, would start some sort of investigation. Instead, all they offered her was a little sympathy, a few patronizing smiles, and empty reassurance. For a fraction of a second, they made her wonder if Kim *could* have gone skiing. Why wouldn't they cooperate? Surely their excuse that they never investigated until a person had been missing for twenty-four hours wouldn't apply to Kim. They all well knew she'd been gone longer, but for some dark reason, they didn't believe she was really missing. She gave a hopeless shake of her head. The "law" in these isolated mountain towns was something else! Maybe it was their way of dealing with the hordes of newcomers who flocked to the ski resorts and ruined the town for the long-time residents. But then a more chilling thought struck her: Was their brushing her off part of a cover-up for something the police had going on the side? Whatever their reason, she was on her own. If any investigating were to be done, she'd have to do it herself.

Furiously she drove back to the chalet. Once inside, she flung her hat and jacket on the couch, then tramped upstairs to the loft.

She would start at the top, searching Kim's armoire.

Methodically she sorted through the hats, scarves, gloves, and purses on the top shelf. A faint fragrance, a woodsy scent that Kim often wore, lingered in the armoire. One by one she went through Kim's clothes hanging on the rack. She recognized most of the skirts, blouses, dresses, and slacks, the "old faithfuls," as Kim called them, the ones she'd worn in New York. A search through the pockets of the few new clothes told her nothing.

The long drawer at the bottom of the armoire was filled with neatly folded socks, tights, leotards, and nylons. Not a clue. For once she wished Kim were not so neat. No odds and ends were tucked away in a corner, no clothes crumpled in a heap. In fact, Kim was the sort of person who believed if she hadn't worn an article of clothing in the past year, she didn't need it, and off it went to the Goodwill. Kelly let out a dispirited sigh. Her search of the armoire told her only one thing: It was impossible to know whether any of Kim's clothes was missing, much less whether she'd packed for a trip.

Resolutely she attacked the dresser, a golden oak antique surmounted by a tall, oval mirror that her thrifty sister must have snapped up at a yard sale. Arranged neatly atop a crisp white runner was an assortment of perfume bottles, a pink plastic bottle of Rose Milk lotion, a Tyrolean music box, and the petit point–covered jewelry box.

Quickly she sorted through the drawers — underwear, nightshirts, warm-up suits — nothing of interest. She slammed the last drawer closed and straightened up, glaring in frustration at the mirror. For a fleeting second it seemed that Kim was gazing back at her. Then, achingly aware that she was staring at her own reflection, Kelly looked away. Her eyes lighted on the music box, a miniature Swiss chalet. She picked it up, wound it, and set it down. The gay, lilting strains of "Blue Danube" poured forth as if in a valiant attempt to cheer her.

Kelly reached for the jewelry box to examine its gold-plated catch. Odd, she thought. Very odd. Kim had never locked it when she lived in the brownstone. Where was the key? She certainly hadn't found it in the armoire or in the dresser. Had Kim taken the key with her? Why hadn't she taken the jewelry? But maybe jewelry had nothing to do with Kim's disappearance. Still puzzled over the locked box, Kelly went downstairs, flicked on the hall light, and opened the closet door.

The closet, a humongous dark cavern where Kim had stored everything else she owned, smelled faintly of mothballs and leather boots. On the shelves on the back wall were stacked brown cardboard cartons labeled Christmas, Summer Shoes, Iced Tea Glasses, along with other cartons containing items Kim seldom used.

The shelves on the left wall were jammed full: bags of rock salt, plastic scrapers; a box of electrical supplies, household tools; sewing needles and spools of thread; a shelf piled with towels, sheets, pillowcases, and blankets; and another completely laden with canned foods. Clearly Kim believed in a well-stocked pantry.

Overhead, on her right, a thick wooden rod packed with sweaters, coats, and jackets stretched from the front of the closet to the rear wall. At the back of the rod hung four long, clear, plastic garment bags stuffed with summer clothes. No need to sort through these, Kelly decided. She tried to shove them back against the end wall, but something was in the way. They were dragging against something resting on the floor in the corner. The hall light didn't quite penetrate to the dark corners of the closet. She dropped to her knees and swept the plastic bags out of the way. Her heart turned over. In the corner, behind the garment bags, stood Kim's matched set of navy blue luggage: a pullman case, a medium-size suitcase, and a cosmetic case.

Stunned, Kelly sat for several moments, trying to absorb the shock of her discovery. Kim hadn't gone away on a trip! At once she began rationalizing. Kim had probably taken along a flight bag, or a backpack — on a short trip she wouldn't need a set of luggage. Kelly clung to the thought, refusing to let herself think any further.

She stood up and flipped through the clothes on the rack: car coats, a black fake fur, an all-weather nutmeg-colored raincoat — She stopped short, uttering a startled exclamation, yanking the hanger from the rod. At last she had found something. "No!" she murmured in a harsh whisper. "It can't be!"

She backed out of the closet and stood under the hall light, holding Kim's pale blue parka at arm's length before her, staring unhappily at the Blue Angel Lodge logo on the front. "This doesn't mean a thing!" she said sharply. She dived back into the closet, parting the clothes where she'd found the parka, and found matching blue ski pants. A knot of anxiety tightened inside her. Until this moment, she hadn't realized how much she had wanted to believe that Kim had gone skiing. She couldn't really believe Kim owned more than one ski outfit — not her penny-wise, non-skiing sister. Dispiritedly, she continued to search through Kim's clothes.

She had almost reached the end of the rod when she heard a door slam, then a loud thumping and bumping. Her hand froze in midair. She was home! Kelly raced into the living room calling, "Kim, Kim, is that you?"

An empty silence eddied around her. Dismayed, she stood stock-still. Suddenly it came again, the loud pounding, from somewhere above and behind her. She started violently and spun around, staring up at the loft. She could see no one. Her gaze shifted down the hallway toward the kitchen. The kitchen door was closed; she'd forgotten to let the cats out when she came home. Had someone broken in the back door? The small voice inside her head prodded, *If you want to know, go open the door!* She couldn't move. *The cats,* she told herself, *the cats have jumped up on the table, knocked something off . . . the sugar bowl . . .*

She took a deep breath and started toward the kitchen. Suddenly, shattering the stillness, a loud, shrill voice shouted, "Hey,

Dad, where's my sleeping bag?" Then a lower, deeper voice answered, "In the van. Go bring it in, and bring Billy's, too."

A hysterical laugh escaped her. Her knees folded beneath her. Weakly she dropped down on the couch. Shaking her head at her own irrational fear, she murmured, "Now I know where you're coming from!"

As she sat quietly, trying to recover her composure, she heard more doors slamming and feet pounding up and down the wooden staircase that paralleled Kim's on the far side of the wall. When she felt calm again, she got to her feet and peered out the window. A forest-green van stood at the curb, glistening in the sunlight. The snow-crusted sidewalk leading to the chalet next door was pockmarked with footprints.

Hastily she threw on her jacket and went next door. A kind-looking man in his forties, wearing a brown jumpsuit and holding a frosty can of Coors, answered her knock. A woman in a red jogging suit stood at his side, warming her hands around a mug of steaming coffee.

Kelly summoned a smile. "I'm sorry to bother you — I'm Kelly Conover from next door."

The man opened the door wide and said pleasantly, "Do come in. I'm Dr. Graham,

81

and this is my wife, Wendy." Two boys clad in jeans and sweatshirts, whom Kelly judged to be about eight and ten, each clutching a mangled sandwich, stood gazing at her with avid interest.

In fond tones, Dr. Graham went on, "And these ruffians are our sons, Dave and Billy." He motioned her inside. "Come in, come in!"

Smiling, Kelly shook her head. "Thanks, but I can't stay." Quickly she told them of her anxiety over Kim, asking if they knew where she might have gone.

"I saw her!" said Dave excitedly. "I saw her last time we were here. She looks just like you."

"Yes, she looks just like me," agreed Kelly. "Tell me when you saw her . . . I mean, when were you here?"

The boy shrugged. Wendy Graham wrinkled her brow. "It must have been at least a month ago."

Dr. Graham gave a judicious nod. "At least. We try to escape Denver twice a month, but we don't always make it."

Kelly shook her head hopelessly. "Everybody's seen her, but nobody knows where she is. The police refuse to start looking for her until tomorrow."

Wendy Graham's soft gray eyes turned

sympathetic. "Have you checked to see if her car is there?"

"Car!" repeated Kelly, as if it were a foreign word. "There was no car parked out front when I got here — and no cleared space where it might have been — so she must have left before the last big snow, more than a week ago."

Billy grinned widely, as if relishing some secret knowledge. "She doesn't drive a car. She drives a neat-looking jeep, dark blue with a light blue canvas top, with R-E-N-E-G-A-D-E printed on the side."

"Renegade," said Dr. Graham. "She drives a Renegade. I suppose you've checked the garage."

"Garage!" exclaimed Kelly. "What garage?"

"Under the chalet, in back," Wendy said. "Behind the kitchen door there's a door that leads downstairs to the garage."

"I saw it, but I thought it was a closet —"

Dr. Graham interrupted. "The ground drops off back of these places and the builder tucked garages underneath. They keep the chalets warmer in the winter — keep our cars from freezing up and being buried in a heavy snow. If you've ever tried to shovel out a car after . . ."

Kelly stopped listening. Mingled hope

and excitement coursed through her. She wished Dr. Graham would stop rambling. Finally she broke in.

"Yes, well, I'll check out the garage. Thanks for the tip." She wheeled and bolted across the yard to Kim's chalet.

Moments later, she raced down the stairs from the kitchen, through the basement and wrenched open the door to the garage. Breathless, she stood on the threshold, staring into the shadowy cavern. In the dusky light that sifted through the window in the overhead door she saw the bulky shape of a jeep. She went numb, staring at it in disbelief. Why she should feel such a sense of shock, she couldn't explain. She supposed, in the back of her mind, she'd thought Kim had taken off under her own power. That her wheels were here only meant she'd gone off with someone else, no more. It could be for the best. If Kim was in trouble, she wasn't alone.

Kelly walked slowly around the jeep, examining it carefully, as if it would give some hint as to Kim's whereabouts. She ambled around to the far side and drew up short. She felt as though her blood were draining from her veins. Hanging from a rack on the wall were a pair of cream-colored skis and poles. On the floor beneath them stood a dark-blue cloth boot bag.

She knelt down, zipped it open, and gazed numbly at Kim's ski boots. With trembling fingers she unzipped the outer compartment and pulled out a pair of dark-blue fleece-lined gloves. She started to stuff them back inside when she noticed a zippered pocket on the back of the left glove. In the pocket she found two keys to the jeep, a credit card, a five-dollar bill, and a card good for ten lessons at Blue Angel Ski School. Hastily, she stuffed keys, credit card, and money into the pocket and dropped the gloves in the boot bag.

Clutching the lesson card, she dashed upstairs to the phone and dialed the number of the Blue Angel Ski School. A harassed-sounding man answered.

Breathless, she said, "May I speak to your ski instructor, please?"

"Which one? We have eight instructors here."

Kelly almost shouted, "Whoever teaches the novice class!"

With barely concealed impatience the voice countered, "Several of our instructors teach novice classes."

"The class Kim Conover is in. Please, it's important."

She heard a weary sigh. "Hold on. I'll look it up."

Kelly held, biting her lip in impatience. Loud music and boisterous laughter sounded in the background. At last the man said flatly, "She's in Eric Brunner's class."

"May I speak to him, please?"

"Sorry, he's out on the slopes." His voice held a note of finality. "You'll have to call back later."

"Wait!" Kelly cried. "When is his class over?"

A vexed sigh burst in her ear. "Four-thirty. Then he usually takes a run or two down the slopes. Sometimes he stops by the lodge, and sometimes he doesn't. Your guess is as good as mine." Before Kelly could question him further, he hung up.

Never had time dragged so slowly, like waiting for an iceberg to melt, thought Kelly wearily. Shortly before four o'clock she swung up the gravel road leading to Blue Angel Lodge. She would find Eric Brunner and catch him before he headed home. As she drove toward the parking area, the blue and white marquee caught her eye. She slammed on the brakes, gaping in astonishment. Splashed across it in huge blue letters were the words: WELCOME K. CONOVER!

Chapter Six

Kelly blinked and looked again. The words were still there, in foot-high letters: **WELCOME K. CONOVER!** She almost cried out with joy and relief. This was someone's idea of a royal welcome home for Kim. She was here! Here in the lodge!

She parked the car and hurried inside. As she'd expected, the après-ski crowd had gathered in the spacious, glass-walled lounge. Her heart hammering with excitement, she stood on tiptoe, searching the throng of faces for Kim. A group of skiers and nonskiing cronies were gathered around a roaring fire that blazed merrily in a massive stone fireplace. At the far end of the room guests were seated on high stools before a long polished mahogany bar, their exuberant faces reflected in the mirror behind it. Others stood in clusters, laughing and chatting, drinking beer or hot buttered rum in shiny silver tankards. In a far corner a buxom girl with rosy cheeks and waist-long brown hair was playing a guitar and singing a folk song in a clear, plaintive voice.

Kelly thought, That's where Kim will be, listening to the guitar player. She wove her way toward the group gathered around the girl. All at once her eyes met and held those of a slender, wiry man of medium height with a broad smile and short curly blond hair, clad in blue ski togs with a Blue Angel Lodge logo. Kelly gave a start. He was the man in Kim's photo. His clear blue eyes widened in astonishment. With rapid strides he elbowed through the crowd and before she could protest, he enfolded her in his arms in a powerful bear hug, then kissed her fervently on each cheek.

Smiling broadly, he said in charmingly accented tones, "I heard you were back." His tone turned reproachful, accusing. "Why did you run off without telling anyone — without telling me? And what have you done to your hair?"

Suddenly self-conscious, she reached up and smoothed the short silken strands. Before she could think of a reply, he went on, gazing at her in mild surprise. "It changes your image; gives you a sophisticated, worldly look. And you've lost weight as well." Then quickly, as if afraid he'd offended her, he said, "It becomes you!"

Kelly felt a chill tingle down her spine. He, too, had mistaken her for Kim. If he thought she was Kim, then Kim wasn't here. A wave of disappointment flowed through her. She shook her head in denial. "Sorry, I'm afraid you've made a mis—"

A high, shrill feminine voice broke in. "Eric, Eric darling. I've been looking everywhere for you!"

Kelly stifled a gasp as a petite, dark-haired girl barged between them, clutching Eric's arm with a proprietary air. Fatuously, she gazed up into his face. "I thought you were lost!" The girl tore her gaze from Eric and turned to level a hostile stare at Kelly from narrow, ice-blue eyes.

Kelly felt the hair bristle on the back of her neck. It was the fox-faced girl who had stared so spitefully at her in the Italian Grotto.

Eric grinned. "I'm never lost, Lauren." His admiring gaze lingered on Kelly. With a sort of courtly, old-world charm, he said, "Isn't Kim's new hairdo terrific? It gives her an altogether different look."

"It's certainly different," said Lauren venomously.

Kelly, suddenly annoyed, feeling like a sheep at a county fair being judged for a blue ribbon, bit her tongue.

Lauren's scarlet lips curved in a frosty smile. "I thought you'd gone back to your sister's in New York."

"Oh?" said Kelly, feigning astonishment, "did I tell you I was going to visit my sister?"

Lauren's face turned crimson, as if she'd been caught in a lie. "Well, no. But now that Eric's taught you to ski, there's no reason for you to stay. I thought you'd finally realized that — and gone back to where you belong."

Eric's blond brows drew together in a slight frown. He flung an arm about Kelly's shoulders in a protective gesture.

"Nonsense." An indulgent smile played at the corners of his mouth. "Kim belongs here as much as any of us — particularly me, an Austrian refugee." He slung his free arm around Lauren's shoulders. "Come on, girls, I'll buy you both a drink."

As he led them toward the bar Kelly's mind seethed with conflicting thoughts. Her first impulse was to tell everyone she met that she was not Kim, had no idea where she was, and ask them to help find her. Now she had second thoughts. Why would Kim leave town without telling anyone? Especially Eric! There must be some good reason why she wanted no one to know she was gone, or where, or why. Did someone here in Blue Angel want her out of the way? Had someone driven her off? If she kept silent, Kelly decided, let everyone think she was Kim, maybe she'd learn something worthwhile.

They perched on high padded red leather stools before the bar, Eric seated between Kelly and Lauren, like the neutral zone in a war-torn country, thought Kelly wryly. At once, Lauren monopolized Eric, resting her pale, slender hand possessively on his arm. If she meant to annoy Kelly, she failed. Kelly was too busy trying to unravel her own tangled thoughts.

She was only vaguely aware that someone had eased onto the empty barstool on her left until a low, sharp voice close to her ear muttered, "Where the hell have you been?"

Her head whipped around and she stared into a pair of close-set, glittering eyes. He was a tall, reedy man with a sharp nose, lean jaw, and a mean, hard look about him. Garbed in a red-and-black-checked flannel shirt and grubby jeans, and a black, broad-brimmed felt hat that shaded his face, he struck her as being out of place in the colorful, fashionably dressed crowd. His thin lips curled in a mocking smile. "I'm glad you're back."

Kelly thought, *You don't look glad.* His snide smile reminded her of a weasel she'd once seen, tearing apart a mouse. He also reminded her of someone else she'd met recently, but before she could recall whom, he went on.

"It's about time you got back. The boss saw your name on the sign out front. You shouldn't have run off like that, without telling anybody. Makes the boss nervous. He wants to see you, now! You'd better see him before he sees you!" He slid from the barstool and slithered away to become lost among the noisy, milling crowd.

Kelly felt a flush of anger surge through her. She'd like to see his boss, *now.* She'd like to ask exactly what business he had to discuss with Kim, but the man had left before she could think of a way to ask who his boss was, without revealing that she wasn't Kim. Obviously, Kim knew exactly who this unsavory character, and his boss, were.

They finished their drinks and ambled over to listen to the folk singer. Several people smiled, speaking to Kelly. She nodded, smiled back, and gave what she prayed were appropriate answers. One of Kim's acquaintances began to question Kelly intently about where she had gone. To escape further awkward questions, Kelly excused herself and fled to the ladies' room.

Around the corner from the cubicles, she

found a wall mirror and sinks where she washed her hands, then brushed her hair. She heard the door open, and the voices of two women talking in low, excited tones, as if telling tales out of school.

Kelly paid no attention until she heard Kim's name mentioned. She continued to stand before the mirror brushing her hair, refreshing her makeup, unashamedly listening.

A low-pitched voice said, "I'm glad she's back."

In gossipy tones a voice replied, ". . . can't believe he'd be taken in by that Duval twit." As if suddenly aware that someone else was in the room, they lowered their voices. Kelly, straining to hear, caught only snatches as they went on.

". . . he and Lauren were a number before Kim Conover . . . dating Kim for weeks . . . why she left town? . . . maybe a lover's quarrel . . . now that she's back, she'll give Lauren Duval a run for her money!" Kelly heard the cubicle doors open and thud shut. Swiftly she rounded the corner, slipped out the door, and rejoined Eric and his friends in the lounge.

She longed to go back to the chalet, but she had to stay, on the chance she'd learn something useful. First, she would check to see who had arranged for the welcome sign on the marquee. But she found the manager's office locked. Resolutely she squared her shoulders, determined to muddle through the evening. She fielded embarrassing questions and asked several of her own, but when the party finally broke up, she had learned nothing new.

Badly shaken, she resolved that if Kim didn't show up by tomorrow morning, she would see Captain Creel and raise such Cain that he would have to start an investigation just to get rid of her and restore order to his department.

It was almost midnight when she pulled up before Kim's chalet, tired and distraught. She was glad she'd remembered to shut the cats in the kitchen, but she wished she had remembered to turn on the lamp in the window before she left. From outside, the dark, draped window gave the place such an ominous air that she hated to enter alone.

Even the moon was hiding behind the clouds. Fumbling in the dark for her key, she jammed it in the lock on the front door. The door swung open. The cats flew out. Kelly gasped. Astonished disbelief, shock, and fear coursed through her in quick succession. If she had locked the cats in the kitchen, and she knew very well she had, who had let them out? Not Kim, that was for sure. If Kim had come home, found her cats and her clothes, she'd know Kelly couldn't be far away — at least she would have left a light on. Suddenly Kelly jumped, startled out of her wits as the cats brushed against her ankles and scurried out of the cold night into the dark chalet.

She stepped inside and closed the door. If someone were here, why were there no lights burning? Could the electricity have been cut off? With the suddenness of a summer storm it struck her. Someone could be standing there in the dark, waiting for Kim. She stood paralyzed, her back flattened against the door, hardly daring to breathe. All she could hear was her heart thudding in her chest. She reached out, her fingers raking the wall for the light switch, and at once thought better of it. If someone were there waiting to pounce on her, why show herself?

She slipped off her shoes and tiptoed down the hall into the kitchen. In the eerie green light of the microwave clock, she made her way to the cabinets. She pulled out a drawer and quietly rummaged through the utensils until her hand closed around the wooden handle of a bread knife. Standing with her back to the wall, she flicked on the light. The kitchen was deserted. Her terrified gaze fixed on the door leading down to the garage. The lock button on the knob was pushed in, just as she'd left it.

Stiffening her spine, she marched down the hall to the closet and yanked open the door. No sinister figure was crouching in the crowded closet, poised to spring out at her. With a show of bravado, she moved on to the bathroom, kicked the door wide, and flipped on the light, her eyes riveted on the stall shower. No dark form loomed behind the frosted glass door. Her breath came out in a rush of relief.

Gripping the knife tightly, she padded past the dining room into the living room and turned on the lamp. The room was empty. Surely if someone were waiting for her, he'd have attacked by now. Reassured, she mounted the stairs to the loft. At the top of the stairs, she stopped stock-still. Her breath caught in her throat. In the faint light filtering up from the living room, she saw a motionless form sprawled on the king-size bed under the quilted spread.

She stifled a joyous cry. Kim! Kim was home at last! Relief flooded through her. She started to wake her, then thought better of it. Kim was probably exhausted. She would let her sleep. Just knowing she was home safe was enough for now. She tossed the knife on a chair. Quietly she undressed and slipped into a pink gown. She eased onto the side of the bed and stretched out on her back under the heavy quilt. Cautiously, she turned her face toward Kim, to make sure she hadn't wakened her. A cry of panic died in her throat. The sleeping figure beside her had short, dark hair and a long, lanky frame that stretched way past hers under the covers.

Stifling a scream, Kelly sat up, whipped the shade off the heavy pottery lamp on the nightstand, and grabbed it by the neck. She rose to her knees, raised the lamp over her head, and with a powerful sweep of her arm slammed it down on the still form beside her.

At the same instant, as if warned of danger by some atavistic instinct, the sleeping figure stirred, rolled out of harm's way and jerked bolt upright in the bed.

An outraged bellow resounded through the silent chalet. "Good Lord, woman, you almost hit me!"

Kelly, still gripping the lamp whose heavy pottery base lay harmlessly on the pillow beside her, sat unmoving, unable to speak, staring down at Brad York.

He gave her shoulder a comforting pat. "Sorry I scared you, sweetie, but I gave up waiting for you to come home."

Kelly, finding her voice, burst out in an indignant shriek. "Brad York! Where did *you* come from?"

A wide grin split his good-natured features. "Actually, I came by way of New York. And since I hadn't heard from you, I thought you might need me. So I hopped in my old reliable ski-equipped superplane, landed on the old airstrip back of the chalets, and here I am!"

"So I see! How did you get in here? It's a wonder the neighbors didn't call the police and report you for breaking and entering."

"Who, me?" said Brad with an injured air. "I wouldn't think of breaking and entering. I used my handy credit card to jimmy the lock. I never leave home without it, and you shouldn't either, sweetie. You just never know . . ."

Kelly narrowed her eyes. "How did you find out where Kim lives?"

Amusement kindled in his dark eyes. "Very easily — from the envelope on one of her letters in your apartment."

"Very enterprising," said Kelly, impressed in spite of herself. "You just lucked out, I suppose, landing in the dark, on her back doorstep."

"Wrong!" replied Brad, smirking. "I arrived before the sun sank over the yardarm. There's a small airport nearby that services feeder lines and private planes for people flying into surrounding ski areas. I talked to your friendly local control tower, got a reading on Alpine Village, and found out it was located beside the old airstrip they used before the new airport was built." His lips curved in an engaging smile. "If I hadn't set down there, I'd have rented a car. Instead I flew to your side like a homing pigeon."

Kelly took a deep breath to strengthen her resolve. "Well, don't think you're going to stay here!"

Brad's dark brows rose in astonishment. "Oh, I had no intention of staying here. I made a reservation for us at Blue Angel Lodge."

"You!" shrieked Kelly. "You had that, that brazen announcement splashed all over the marquee! *Welcome K. Conover!*"

With cheerful goodwill, he replied, "I thought it was a nice touch. You know my motto: It pays to advertise."

Indignation surged through her. "I know your motto, and I know *you*, Brad York. And

I'm not staying with you at Blue Angel Lodge."

Brad raised his hands as if fending off an attack. "I only made a reservation for us in case Kim already had a roommate. When I discovered you and Kim were both out, I decided to wait here for you."

"In bed!" shouted Kelly. "Did you have to wait in my bed?"

"I can't think of a better place. Can you?"

"Yes. The lodge. You haul your body out of my bed and hotfoot it back there!"

"On foot?" Brad exclaimed. "Out of the question. I'm really not dressed to go out in the cold." He flung back the blanket, revealing a broad, furred chest; narrow hips, and lean, hairy, muscular legs. Before she could speak, he went on. "Anyway, Kim's side of the bed is free, obviously. Where *is* your sweet beautiful sister, better known as good old Kim?"

At the mention of Kim's name, Kelly's throat constricted and tears sprang to her eyes. "Oh, Brad, I'm worried half out of my mind about her. She isn't here — hasn't been here since I don't know when. She's disappeared."

"Disappeared!" echoed Brad incredulously. "Nobody simply disappears." He reached out and clasped her shoulders in a reassuring squeeze. "You can stop worrying, my love. I'll help you find her. You're lucky I came. I *knew* you needed me!"

"I do *not* need you!" shouted Kelly, feeling irritated and frustrated at the same time. "We're finished, Brad. *Finished!* Why won't you believe me? What must I do to prove it?"

Unperturbed, his hands still on her shoulders, he gazed deeply into her eyes and gave an eloquent sigh. "I'm afraid that's one of those things in life that are impossible to prove." His hands slid down her arms, and up again, over her shoulders, resting on either side of her face. He bent his head and kissed her lightly on the mouth.

She tried to push him away. His hands captured hers. He lifted them to his lips and kissed first one palm, then the other.

"The truth is, I missed you like blazes."

She disengaged her hands from his grasp. "You can't miss me. It's against the rules."

Gently his fingers trailed over her face, stroked her hair, caressed the back of her neck. A tender smile curved his mouth. "All right, my independent lady, let's just say I want to ski in Colorado. I've never skied in Colorado." He leaned forward and kissed her lightly on the lips.

She drew away from him. Briskly she said,

"It's time you were on your way. Get up and get dressed." Struck with an idea, she went on. "You must be starving. I'll fix you something to eat, and then drive you to the lodge."

Brad put his arms around her, pulling her close, nibbling her earlobe. "I've had something to eat. I raided your fridge. And by the way, your watch-cats are no protection at all. As a matter of fact, I bribed them with hamburger. But I'm still hungry. Man cannot live by bread alone." He pulled her tightly against his chest and his lips claimed hers in an ardent, demanding kiss that left her breathless and shaking. His warm, strong hands ran down her back, pressing her slender figure firmly to his. Involuntarily her hands traveled over the familiar curves of his body, reveling in the feel of his long, muscular frame, the familiar starchy scent of him. He murmured the endearments she so loved to hear. Her body molded to his.

With a supreme effort of will, she pushed him away.

"Brad, you really have to go."

His lips close to her ear sent shivers tingling down her spine. "I don't know how to tell you this, my love, but it's too late. The desk clerk said if I didn't check in by six they'd give the room to someone else."

He was lying, of course. She was sure he'd already checked in, probably at the same time he'd conned the manager into putting **WELCOME K. CONOVER** on the marquee; and she knew from past experience it did no good to argue with Brad York. With her last ounce of willpower, Kelly whispered, "Then you'll have to find another place to stay."

"I will, darling, don't worry. First thing in the morning." His lips captured hers, silencing further protests.

Chapter Seven

Kelly awoke the next morning shortly before seven, feeling marvelous. Drowsily she yawned, stretched, and from force of habit glanced at the space beside her to see if Kim had come home. Kim wasn't there. Brad was. Her feeling of euphoria evaporated. This beguiling man seemed ever-present, popping up like a dandelion in the smooth lawn of her existence. The only thing to do was ignore him — show him once and for all that she could get along without him very well. This morning, when Captain Creel came on duty, Kelly would be there waiting for him, to file a missing person's report — without any help from Brad York.

Brad lay on his back, breathing deeply and evenly, a contented half-smile lingering on his lips. Her heart turned over as she watched him, her gaze roving over his tousled, curly black hair, thick black brows, straight nose, and wide, generous mouth. How could anyone who looked so innocent,

so harmless, be such a devil on wheels, de-
molish all her best intentions, wind her
around his little finger like a wisp of yarn?
She had enough problems without Brad
around to complicate her life. She had fled
to Colorado in part to escape him, and escape him she would. He would have to go.

She hated losing such a close friend. She
felt she had known Brad all her life, when in
fact they'd met only three months ago,
skiing at Sugarloaf Mountain in Vermont.
With a twinge of nostalgia she recalled that
Saturday evening when the après-ski crowd
had gathered in the lodge, Brad strolling in,
ruddy-cheeked, and smiling, a devilish glint
in his dark eyes, to mingle with the skiers.

At once an air of excitement and tension
seemed to invade the room. Women hov-
ered about him like hummingbirds sipping
nectar from a flower. With detached amusement Kelly had watched him gaze into the
eyes of every woman he spoke to as if she
were the only woman in the world. How ur-
bane, witty, and insinuatingly sensual he
was! She smothered a grin. Men like Brad
meant big trouble. She wouldn't touch him
with a six-foot ski pole!

As the evening wore on, Brad detached
himself from a flock of admiring females
and strode to her side.

"I was irresistibly drawn to you," he said, giving her an intimate, lopsided grin.

Immediately she was on guard against him, against letting herself be mesmerized by the man's undeniable charm. She eyed him coldly. She suspected he was one of those men who required the adulation of every woman in the room, and now he wanted to make sure she, too, worshipped him as he deserved.

The minute he opened his mouth, he was off on the wrong foot with her. When he asked where she worked, she told him, with a small show of pride, that she had started her own business, Conover Executive Suites. His mouth widened in a facetious grin. "Is that spelled S-W-E-E-T-S?"

Cool and unsmiling, Kelly spelled the name. Her icy manner quickly dissolved, overridden by enthusiasm as she explained that her company leased or purchased suites of offices and equipment, then offered space, use of the equipment, and secretarial services to businesses that needed temporary offices in New York City.

She saw a gleam of interest light his eyes, mingled with something like approval and respect. She could almost see him regroup. From that moment on he plainly showed he thought she was a woman who knew where she was going — a fascinating female worth listening to. Less than an hour after her stern warning to beware of smooth talkers with swift lines, her heart was racing faster than a skier on a downhill run.

Every time she and Brad met it seemed as though they struck sparks that ignited like wildfire. Brad had designed a brochure for Executive Suites that caught on like wildfire as well. All the while Kelly kept telling herself that theirs was a business relationship, nothing more. He'd followed up his direct mail blitz with an intriguing billboard ad near the airport. Not content, he'd set about placing short articles about Kelly, an up-and-coming young businesswoman, in trade journals and house organs, until finally she'd had to call a halt. He was so eager to please her, to see her succeed, that without realizing it he was taking over her business. Gently but firmly she'd told him that sometimes you can give a person more help than she wants. It was, after all, *her* business, and she had to prove that she could make a success of it. To Kelly's relief, Brad eased up on her business interests, only to redouble his efforts to capture her heart. She backed off. But it seemed that the faster she ran, the harder he chased her.

Brad had claimed they were meant for

each other. Kelly, eyeing him with a fond, skeptical smile, had agreed only that they had much in common, particularly their enthusiasm for skiing. She had loved flying off in Brad's twin-engine Beechcraft for skiing weekends in Vermont, and though she had vowed no man would ever be the center of *her* world, she had found it exciting and thrilling to be the center of *his* world. Nothing in her life had been the same since she'd met Brad York.

A wistful smile curved her lips. Too bad her merry-go-round life with Brad had to end. But what a relief it would be to escape his persuasive charm. She had given up trying to make him understand that she wasn't ready to settle down to marriage. Fiercely independent, she had a horror of being tied down. The husbands she knew were always telling their wives what to do. "Marriage!" she scoffed. "Who needs it!"

Last Monday, suddenly obsessed with the need to drive to Colorado to find Kim, she had told him a final "No!" Her face flamed as she recalled her harsh words. Feeling like Scrooge, she'd told him this was his big chance to find someone else, that he'd better take advantage of it. Then she'd tossed her clothes into a suitcase, gathered up her stray cats, and bolted out of town.

Would he take advantage of it, she now wondered, find someone else? Unaccountably, as she lay there smiling at him, her heart gave a painful wrench.

But it was no good lying here, letting her mind wander. She had things to do. She wished it weren't too early to catch the reluctant Captain Creel. Quietly she slid from the bed and dressed, pulling on warm gray slacks and a heavy tan turtleneck sweater. Her mind churned. There had to be something else she could do to track Kim down. By the time she'd finished breakfast, talking to herself, she knew what it was. "Better take Kim's jeep," she murmured. "The Mustang is low on gas, and who knows how far away this place is."

Ten minutes later, armed with Kim's map, she was tooling up into the foothills of Blue Angel Mountain toward the site of the Alpenstock Land Development Corporation properties. Maybe there she would find the elusive Mr. Teague. Her heart gave an optimistic leap. Maybe she would find Kim!

The air was crisp and clear, the sky a deep blue. The distant soft blue mountain ranges, rock-ribbed barriers lined with virgin snow, thrust into a cloudless sky, their summits wreathed in early-morning mist.

She guided the jeep down the gravel road

past low pinon- and juniper-covered hills for several miles before she realized she was slowly climbing. Soon pinon and juniper were replaced by open, snow-clad hillsides dotted with ranches where white-faced Herefords grazed. Mingled excitement and anticipation churned inside her as the jeep roared along the winding road. As she rounded a curve the river came into view, wide, shining, struck with silver in the early morning sunlight. She gazed at it in delight. Her delight soon dissolved into disgust as she passed large dredging piles of boulders and gravel where the riverbed had been scooped up, sifted for gold, then dumped, leaving ugly scars.

Ten minutes later she spotted a green and white **ALPENSTOCK CONDOS** sign with an arrow pointing the way down a narrow, rocky dirt road carved through the foothills. Kelly swung right. The jeep jounced along for two more miles when the road came to an abrupt end. Kelly cut the engine and sat staring about her in amazement. Though Kim had told her that Mr. Teague's development was situated on the site of an abandoned mine, she had interpreted "abandoned" to mean "gone." She couldn't have been more wrong.

An eerie feeling crept through her as her

gaze traveled over a tall heavy-timbered structure that looked for all the world like a gallows. At its base sprawled a long, decrepit, rotting wood building with a rusted, corrugated metal roof. Nearby stood a tall weathered building with chutes along the base, like wide open mouths.

Her gaze traveled on past a broken-down wagon with two missing wheels that made it list like a foundered ship. Her attention shifted to the track that wound up a slight slope and ended a hundred yards away in front of a huge dilapidated Victorian house. Her spirits sank. The place looked deserted.

Kelly got out of the car and, tucking her scarf more tightly about her neck, trudged toward the house. As she tramped past the long shed, the side of the house came into view. Parked beside a bay window was a shiny black van with the license tag **SMYTHE**. A wisp of smoke trailed from the chimney. Someone was here after all, she thought, elated. A shiver of anticipation coursed through her.

She paused to survey the house which she guessed must once have belonged to the mine owner or superintendent. At one time it had been painted a warm, brick red with moss-green trim; now it was faded, giving it a lonely and desolate appearance. The third story of the many-gabled mansion boasted a hexagonal tower topped by a spire. Her gaze swept down past the second story with tall narrow windows overlooking a broad porch roof surmounted by a decorative iron railing. On the first floor a short flight of steps led across the porch to the shadowed doorway. Dark green shades, drawn behind the beveled glass door, gave the house a forbidding air.

Kelly took a deep breath to steady her resolve. If Mr. Teague didn't know where Kim was, she'd insist that he help find her. She mounted the steps, crossed the veranda to the glass door, and stopped short. A sign hanging inside the door read: **ALPENSTOCK CONDOS. OFFICE HOURS** 9:00–5:00.

Disconcerted at being put off further, Kelly glanced at her watch. Eight-thirty. There was no use antagonizing the man by rousting him out before office hours. She turned and retraced her steps. Curious, she surveyed the derelict mine. She had never seen a mine — it might be interesting to explore. At least inside the building she'd be out of the wind. Intrigued, she quickened her steps.

If there had been a door, it was long since gone. She stepped inside the long, wide shed, straining to see in the dim gray light that filtered through dirt-encrusted windows high up in the walls. She wrinkled her nose at a dank, damp smell like rotting wood mixed with a strong, gamy odor. Birds had nested under the eaves, and feathers and droppings littered the floor. At the far end of the shed was strewn a pile of two-foot-thick timbers. Beams for supporting the tunnels, she guessed. Walking on, she found herself in a room filled with ancient machinery coated with dust and bound with lacy cobwebs. A small black shape swooped out of the shadows, skimming past her face. She screamed, hiding her head in her arms as the creature dived past her again, then disappeared into the shadows.

"A bat! That's all it is!" she told herself shakily. "Harmless, perfectly harmless. More afraid of you than you are of it." Still, she could do without a run-in with a bat. She backed quickly out of the room and hurried on past what appeared to have been a blacksmith's shop with rusty horseshoes strewn about the base of a sturdy old anvil, and a furnace whose fires had died years ago.

She tripped, almost fell, then, clutching an upright timber, regained her balance. She looked down. She had tripped over a narrow iron track. Curious, she followed it to an open shaft that looked to be about eight feet wide and sixteen feet long. Cautiously she braced one hand against a beam and peering down into the dark seemingly bottomless shaft, saw the sheen of water. A shudder shook her as she envisioned miners descending in the cagelike elevator to tunnels buried hundreds of feet in the bowels of the earth, coming up again bringing supplies and ore to the surface. To someone like herself, who could scarcely endure the thought of being tied down, it would be a living death.

She had no idea how long she had been standing there staring down the shaft when she had the feeling she was being watched. Gooseflesh prickled her skin. Slowly she turned her head.

At the same moment a voice from the shadows snarled, "What the hell are you doing snooping around here?"

Startled half out of her wits, she teetered on the edge of the shaft, then clutched the wooden support beam with both hands, bracing herself against it. She wheeled to face a man wearing a faded denim jacket and grubby jeans. He glared at her malevolently through yellow-tinted sunglasses.

Fear closed her throat. She stood staring at him in stunned silence. Now she knew where she'd seen him before. He and his companion had swooped past her on the ski slope, gawking at her in surprise; he was the same disagreeable man who had accosted her the night before at the lodge and tried to frighten her with his threats.

He pushed his sunglasses back on his head and fixed her with narrowed, glittering, coal-black eyes. A thin weasel-like smile twisted his lips. "Cat got your tongue?" Without warning he stepped to her side, grabbed her arm in a viselike grip, and shook her.

Her heart seemed to stop beating. Suddenly enraged, she cried out, "Let go of me!" She tried to wrench from his grasp and jerk away from the edge of the shaft, but his grip on her arm tightened as he held her captive before him.

Angrily he shouted, "You don't fool Bill Smythe with your short hairdo and city clothes, you stupid broad! I know who you are. Kim told us she had a twin sister, and Kim's flown the coop. I've been watching her house, waiting for her to come back — saw you cruising around in your convertible. And you won't fool Clark Teague, either. He's out looking for your thieving sister."

Kelly's mouth dropped open, but no sound came out.

He gave a nasty laugh. "You're the one who got fooled, *sister.* Now you listen to me, and listen good. If you want to stay healthy, you'll see that Kim Conover hands back everything she stole from Clark Teague."

"My sister didn't steal anything!"

"The hell she didn't! And in case nobody told you, stealing is a crime. So don't play innocent with me!"

Faintly, in the distance, Kelly heard a car churning up the road. A coil of fear tightened inside her. Was it the man Teague coming back?

In a voice that shook, she yelled, "I don't know what you're talking about!"

"Well, you damn sight better find out fast, and return everything she made off with, or you're going to be one more mining casualty." He jiggled her arm roughly, as if to thrust her over the edge of the yawning shaft.

She let out a frightened gasp.

His close-set black eyes glittered dangerously. "What's the matter?" he taunted. "Afraid I'll pitch you over?"

Kelly went rigid. "You do, and you'll never get Clark Teague's property back." The next instant she thought she heard a car door slam. Maybe it wasn't Teague, she thought, hope rising inside her. Maybe it was a customer. But a customer wouldn't come to the mine. He'd go up to the house, to the office. Her breath caught in her throat.

Smythe glared at her through narrowed lids. "Then you just tell me where to find your sister. Don't give me that rot about how she's gone on a cross-country ski tour. Teague already sent me off to find her on the damn cross-country and somehow she got away. Now you tell me where she is."

For a fraction of a second Kelly's fear of this madman was overridden by relief that he couldn't find Kim. Furiously she spat, "I don't know where my sister is."

Enraged, his voice rose to a bellow. "You're lying! You tell me where that thieving broad is, or I'll . . ." He gave her a violent shake.

Defiantly Kelly shouted, "If you kill me, or Kim, you'll never get your property back!" In the split second of silence, she thought she heard footsteps approaching. Smythe ranted on.

His thin lips curled in a superior, sinister smile. "If you and your sister are dead, it won't matter!"

The sound of footsteps grew louder, pounding along the frozen ground. Kelly's heart leaped to her throat. It must be Teague after all.

Smythe, still gripping Kelly's arm, wheeled around just as a dark, parka-clad figure hurtled through the doorway. He stopped stock-still. His sharp, appraising gaze traveled swiftly over the two of them, zeroing in on Smythe's hand gripping Kelly's arm. As though shot by an arrow, Smythe's hand dropped to his side.

Before Kelly could speak, he said in cool, superior tones, "Good morning. Am I too late for the morning mine tour?" Pleasantly he went on, "If you've finished, I want to talk to someone about buying a condo."

Kelly thought she would faint. Whether from relief, astonishment, or shock at the way Brad York had just walked in and taken command, she couldn't have said.

Smythe's lips carved in an ingratiating smile. "Be right with you. Miss Conover is just leaving." Turning to Kelly, he said in hard, flat tones, "You do what I told you. I'll deal with you later."

Kelly felt her cheeks burning. Not daring to look at Brad, she fled from the mine, across the snow-crusted ground, back to Kim's jeep. Her Mustang was parked beside it. Brad must have heard her backing the jeep from the garage and followed her up here. Quickly she climbed into the jeep, started the engine, and roared down the road toward home. Brad could take care of himself, no doubt about that, she thought, grinning to herself. You had to get up early in the morning to get ahead of Brad York. But she *had* gotten up early in the morning, and still she wasn't ahead of him!

As she neared town her first impulse was to drive straight to the police station. But Smythe had said something about Kim going on a cross-country tour. Maybe she *had* gone on a cross-country ski trip. Maybe the trip was over. First she'd check the chalet. Maybe Kim was home!

Chapter Eight

As Kelly let herself inside the chalet, silence pressed around her, seeming to squeeze the breath from her lungs. Only the cats rushed out to greet her, howling their hunger. She felt utterly deflated. If she had doubted it before, she now knew for certain that Kim was in serious trouble. Had she really stolen something from this man Teague? Kelly couldn't believe it. No matter! If Kim had stolen the crown jewels of England, Kelly would defend her. But first she had to find her. She would feed the cats, then drive into town to see Captain Creel.

Kelly had no more set the cats' food on the floor than Brad burst through the front door looking angry and upset. At the sight of her, his features relaxed in a relieved grin. He strode into the kitchen and put his arms around her.

"Thank God, you're okay!" His chin nuzzled her hair. "I heard the garage door go up, heard you roar out of here in the jeep at some ungodly hour, so I followed you. What the devil was that all about?"

Kelly disengaged herself from his encircling arms and, planting her hands on her hips, looked up into his face with a firm, direct gaze. "Brad, I can handle this. I don't want you to get involved. I want you out of my life."

Brad's dark, deep-set eyes locked with hers. "If you're in some kind of trouble, I'm going to help."

Suddenly she felt driven to the wall. Her frustration and worry over Kim erupted in anger. "I don't want your help! Don't want you tracking me like a — a hound dog!"

"Hold it!" Brad shouted. "If I hadn't followed you this morning, you could be lying at the bottom of the Blue Angel mine shaft in a watery grave."

"Wrong!" Kelly snapped. "My life wasn't in danger for one second. That creep Smythe was only trying to frighten me into returning whatever it is he thinks Kim stole, or telling him where she is so he can frighten her into returning it."

Brad's dark brows drew together in a scowl. "Then we'd better find Kim before he does."

"Not *we*, Brad, *me*. I'm going to the police.

If anyone can find her, they can."

"Don't bet on it."

Kelly's voice tightened in exasperation. "Listen, Brad, your being here only creates more problems. Can't you see that?" She paused. What she couldn't say was that Brad's presence rattled her beyond reason, aroused feelings of longing and desire she was trying hard to suppress. He cocked his head, regarding her with an air of mystified innocence, as if trying to fathom a completely illogical statement. Forcefully she went on.

"You're acting as though nothing has happened between us, that nothing is settled, when in fact our so-called romance is over, finished, done!" Her voice didn't sound as convincing as she wished, and as he stood watching her, waiting patiently for her to finish, she felt she may as well have been talking to a statue.

Distraught, her voice rose. "I'm going to the police to report what happened in the mine and to tell them Kim is definitely missing." She brushed past him and started out the door.

"I'll go with you."

She whirled to face him. In low, tight tones, she said, "You will not go with me! I'm going alone."

"You're right. I'd better stay here."

"Wrong! I've asked you to leave. Now please go!"

Smiling, he shook his head. "No can do, my love. Suppose Kim tries to phone you in New York? Your secretary will tell her you're here. Then Kim will phone here and . . ."

He had her pinned; she hadn't thought of that. A reluctant sigh escaped her. "Okay, stay here. But as soon as I get back, you're moving on!"

He said nothing. The corners of his mouth curved upward in an impacable smile.

Tense, hopeful, Kelly sat across from Captain Creel's desk, waving away a haze of cigar smoke and waiting for him to tell her what he was going to do.

He leaned back in his swivel chair, gazing at her from under narrowed lids. The entire time she had been pouring out all the reasons she knew Kim was missing and all the events that led up to her confrontation with Smythe in the mine, he'd had a wary, appraising look on his face. Now he let his chair down with a thud. Placing his hands flat on his desk, he leaned forward, regarding her with an intense gaze.

"I sympathize with you, Miss Conover,

understand your concern. But *you* must understand that Mr. Teague is an important man in this town, an upstanding and respected citizen: president of the Chamber of Commerce, member of the Rotary, church deacon, sings in the choir, not to mention that he's a big contributor to the church as well as to the historic society and other worthwhile organizations."

"It sounds as though he has his finger in every pie in town," said Kelly uneasily.

A respectful, almost reverent expression came over the captain's countenance. "And that's without saying all he's done for this town businesswise. Put Blue Angel back on her feet, building all those condos." He paused, drawing deeply on his cigar, as if giving Kelly time to consider his words.

But her only thought was: What's this man Teague done for you? Most of the old-timers here resented new blood. Clearly Captain Creel didn't resent Teague, even though the captain had said Teague was a newcomer. Why should he resent *her?* Why drag his feet about helping her?

He blew a circle of smoke ceilingward, then fixed her with a hard, level stare. "The fact is, you had an argument with Bill Smythe. He didn't attack you, or harm you, and you personally have never heard Clark

Teague threaten your sister."

"But Smythe told me that he —"

Captain Creel interrupted. "You've admitted the man was only trying to scare you, and if your sister *has* stolen something —"

"She hasn't!" Kelly burst out. "Kim would never steal anything from anyone!"

He flicked an ash from his cigar into a black onyx tray. In tones she felt dismissed her just as lightly, he went on. "All right, Miss Conover. We'll make inquiries, and let your sister speak for herself." He stood up to indicate the interview was at an end. "As soon as we find out anything, we'll let you know."

Feeling more depressed and discouraged than she had when she first walked through the door, Kelly thanked Captain Creel and left. At least he'd let her file a missing person's report, she thought grimly. If she didn't hear from him soon, she'd be back on his doorstep, demanding he take further action.

She drove slowly out of town, trying to think what she could do to find Kim, and how she could convince Brad he had to leave. Occupied with her thoughts, she was only vaguely aware that someone was headed down the road behind her. As she steered the jeep around a long, winding curve, she glanced in the rearview mirror. The road was deserted. Odd that anyone should be driving out of town at ten in the morning. Most people headed toward town, or toward the slopes, at a much earlier hour. Whoever it was must have run into town on an errand and had now turned off onto one of the narrow spurs that led to isolated cabins or A-frames studding the steep slope of the mountain on her left. On her right, the road wound past a turquoise lake where a high embankment dropped sharply down to the water's edge. From the corner of her eye, she caught a movement reflected in its tranquil, mirrorlike surface.

She turned her head slightly and gave a start. Rounding the curve she had just passed was a black van. She pressed down on the accelerator, keeping one eye on the rearview mirror. Moments later, she saw the van nosing around a curve behind her. The driver, who had been some distance away, now speeded up, as if to keep her in sight. Strange that he hadn't passed her. She was only going twenty miles an hour. The narrow curving road was strewn with loose gravel. Maybe he thought it was dangerous to pass. Still, she felt uneasy.

She pressed harder on the gas pedal. The needle on the speedometer jumped to thirty.

The black van continued to gain on her, pressing closer and closer until it seemed to be climbing up the back of the jeep. She stared into the mirror, trying to see who was driving, but sunlight glinting off the van's windshield blinded her. The memory of Smythe's black van parked before the Alpenstock office surfaced. Was this Smythe, out to scare her? There were plenty of other black vans in town. It could be anyone — someone tired of poking along behind her, anxious to pass. Why didn't he pass? she wondered nervously.

Kelly accelerated. The van accelerated, too, moving up on her left, inching closer. Her heart pounded, her gloved hands grew hot and damp with fear. He was trying to crowd her off the road! Her glance darted toward the embankment on her right, and a swift vision of the canvas-topped jeep tumbling down the steep hillside into the lake flashed through her mind. She felt a slight jar as the van closed in, nudging the jeep. Terrified, she floored the gas pedal, shooting ahead of the van. Praying no one was coming the other way, she spun the wheel sharply, careening to the left side of the road.

She heard her pursuer gun the motor and the squeal of tires as he veered left, but before he could pull up beside her she shot ahead of him and swerved into the right-hand lane. In the sideview mirror she glimpsed the driver. A giant hand seemed to squeeze her heart. It was Smythe tailgating the jeep.

She felt the jeep rock as he hit the back bumper. Frantically she spun the wheel left, trying to outmaneuver him. Panic rose in her throat. Desperately she clung to the wheel. She couldn't keep up this dodge'em game much longer. Bracing her back against the seat, she gripped the wheel tighter, swung sharply to her right, and slammed on the brake. The van, trying to follow, curved widely to the right, skidded on the gravel, and overshot the jeep. Before Smythe could back up, Kelly spun the wheel in a tight U-turn and charged down the road toward town.

She zoomed around a curve. Though she could no longer see the van, she could hear it roaring down the road after her. She'd never make it all the way back to town. He would catch up with her and then . . . She couldn't bear thinking about it. Desperately she scanned the roadside looking for an escape route, but she knew there were no roads leading anywhere off this one. The road straightened briefly. She glanced in the rearview mirror and her hands froze to the wheel. The black van was charging around the curve, bearing down on her.

She floored the gas pedal, her eyes riveted on the bend ahead. Moments later Smythe was out of sight. She took a deep breath. Just ahead on her right, she saw a wide gash in the trees, a firebreak. At the top of the incline under sheltering pines stood a sprawling L-shaped cabin. It was worth a try. She jammed on the brake, slowed, then spun the wheel to her right. The jeep careened into the lane and, bucking and coughing, struggled up the rough track.

She plunged the gearshift into low. The jeep jerked forward, chugging up the long, sloping hillside, bouncing over ruts, slipping, sliding, dislodging stones, hugging the rugged lane hacked out of the pine forest.

She was halfway up the slope when she heard a screech of brakes, the roar of the van backing up. Blast! He'd seen her! Would he try to follow her up here? Shakily she told herself the van would never make it. She could hear the van's steel-belted tires digging into the road crusted over with ice. Stubbornly she pushed on, up the rough incline. Her fingers felt glued to the wheel. Every muscle in her body ached with tension. Just when she thought she would never reach the top, the ground leveled off and she emerged into a clearing before the cabin. Her hopes plummeted. The place looked deserted. No car stood in the driveway. A neatly lettered wooden sign was stuck in the ground: RUSSELL'S HAVEN — ROOMS TO LET.

She cut the engine, jumped from the jeep, and looked down at the road below. Her breath caught in her throat. The van's wheels were spinning, stalled near the foot of the slope. Smythe gunned the motor. Breathlessly she turned and ran toward the cabin. If only she could get inside, maybe she'd be safe.

She dashed to the door and jabbed at the bell. Gasping for breath, she peered through a small, diamond-shaped window, her hand on the doorknob. Somewhere a dog barked. The door swung open. A plump elderly woman, with bright blue eyes and faded blonde hair pinned in a neat, round bun atop her head, eyed Kelly curiously.

Breathlessly, Kelly said, "I'm Kelly Conover, Mrs. Russell —"

The woman smiled. "I'm not Mrs. Russell. I'm Ida Swenson, the housekeeper." She gave a regretful shake of her head. "The Russells are in town, running some errands."

Nervously Kelly glanced over her shoulder. From here she couldn't see the foot of the firebreak, but she hadn't heard the van drive away. No doubt Smythe had settled down in his van to wait her out, she thought grimly. Disconcerted, she turned back to Ida Swenson. "It's very important that I see Mrs. Russell. May I wait inside?"

Mrs. Swenson nodded agreeably. "They'll be home soon."

Kelly bolted through the doorway into a rustic-looking room boasting heavy, nubby-gold upholstered furniture, Navajo rugs, and hanging brass lamps. In one corner, in a white birdcage, two finches were chirping a cheerful song.

Ida Swenson led her to the couch set before a wide picture window. She pointed to a stretch of road visible through a break in the trees. "From here, you'll be able to see the car turning up the lane to the cabin." Then staring at the jeep, eyeing the tire tracks, she exclaimed, "You drove up the firebreak?"

Kelly's mouth went dry. She gave what she hoped was an unconcerned shrug, hoping Ida Swenson wouldn't question her further.

Mrs. Swenson's bright blue eyes widened with curiosity. "Don't you know that there's a gravel lane farther down the road that leads up to the back of the cabin?" Sudden doubt clouded her eyes. "Why did you drive up the firebreak?"

Kelly sighed inwardly. She'd have to tell her after all. Though she hated to alarm this kind, trusting soul, Kelly quickly explained how Smythe had tried to run her off the road and was waiting at the bottom of the hill for her to come down. Mrs. Swenson sank onto the couch beside her, hearing her out. Sheepishly Kelly confessed that she hadn't really known about this place, that she had been desperate to escape Smythe, find a safe haven, and had pretended she needed to see Mrs. Russell because she'd been afraid Mrs. Swenson wouldn't let her inside the house.

A glimmer of suspicion shone from Ida Swenson's eyes. "Can't you drive away, down the lane back of the cabin?"

Kelly shook her head. "He can see the jeep. And he knows this road well. If I drive away, he'll be there, at the end of the lane, waiting for me."

Suspicion faded from Ida Swenson's eyes, replaced by quick sympathy as she regarded Kelly's ashen face, the stricken look of a trapped animal in her eyes. "My dear, of course you're welcome to stay." Her eyes hardened, her jaw set. "When developers descend on a town like Blue Angel, you never know what sort of people they hire on or lure into town to play at their resorts — strangers clogging the roads, stirring up trouble for us old-timers." Shaking her head, she went on, "A fine world we live in when a body can't even feel safe in a peaceful mountain town!" She hoisted her plump body up off the couch. "Well, you're safe here. When Mr. Russell gets back, he'll run the man off and see you home. Now I'll make you some hot chocolate."

As Mrs. Swenson left for the kitchen, Kelly turned to face the window, staring out over the snowy hillside until her eyes stung. She had neither seen nor heard a car, nor the van, pass along the stretch of road visible through the break in the trees.

As if on cue, Smythe's lean, denim-clad figure topped the rise. Kelly gasped, feeling her skin prickle. Before she could move from the window, she felt the impact of his beady, close-set eyes staring at her through his yellow-tinted glasses. He raised a fist in a menacing gesture and strode rapidly toward the cabin.

Kelly jumped up from the couch and fled to the kitchen, shouting, "Mrs. Swenson, he's here! He's coming after me!"

Without saying a word, Ida Swenson

yanked open a drawer and curved the palm of her hand snugly around the handle of a meat cleaver. She strode from the kitchen. Kelly heard her brisk steps halt before the front door. In the tense silence, a loud ticking sound pounded in her ears with the force of a pickax striking rock. Her glance shifted to a cuckoo clock hanging on the kitchen wall. A loud thumping on the front door made her jump.

Kelly tiptoed to the kitchen door and peeked around the frame, her gaze riveted on the window. Through the diamond-shaped glass she could see Smythe's flushed, angry face. His eyes behind the amber sunglasses swept the room.

"Who is it?" demanded Mrs. Swenson in strident tones.

"Bill Smythe. I want to see Mr. Russell."

Kelly's heart sank. Did he *know* the Russells?

Mrs. Swenson rested the shining blade in the palm of her hand as if testing it. "He's not here. Come back later."

Kelly felt her knees grow weak. Oh no! she thought. Now he knows we're here alone!

Smythe managed an ingratiating smile. "I want to see the rooms he has to rent."

"They're both taken," shouted Mrs. Swenson through the door. She slid the safety chain into the brass slot.

"I sent my wife up here to ask about a room. She must be walking up the lane back of the house. If you don't mind, I'll come in and wait for her." The brass doorknob rattled loudly as he gave it a vigorous twist.

Mrs. Swenson stood on tiptoe, glaring through the glass at Smythe. "Yes, I do mind!" she said in loud, irritated tones. "I'm busy. Anyway, your wife isn't here. You get along and meet her on the driveway, or I'll sic the dog on you!"

Scowling furiously, he turned his head this way and that, peering downward as if to see the dog, trying to gauge its size and strength.

Mrs. Swenson wheeled about, pressed her back flat against the door, lifted her chin, and let out a blood curdling howl that made Kelly's hair stand on end. The face in the window vanished. Mrs. Swenson rose on tiptoe and peered out the window. She let out a peal of laughter. "My land, he's flying down that hill like a jackrabbit bolting for cover!"

Weak with relief, Kelly flopped down on the couch. Thinking of the narrowness of her escape, as if in delayed reaction she began to shake and couldn't stop.

Ida Swenson eyed her sympathetically. "I

think he's decided to leave. Now we'll have our hot chocolate." She disappeared into the kitchen.

Kelly rose to her knees and turned to face the window. Narrowing her eyes against the brilliant sunlight, she scanned the tall furry pines surrounding the house. Was Smythe hiding among the trees, waiting to jump out and capture her — or worse? There wasn't a sign of him to mar the peaceful, white, Christmas-card landscape.

The sound of an engine starting up shattered the silence. Kelly focused her gaze on the empty stretch of road far below. Within seconds, she saw the van careening around the bend, burning rubber. She let out her breath in a rush of relief. Apparently Smythe had lost patience and had given up, but her feelings of relief soon dissolved for he was still out there, somewhere, out to get Kim, and herself as well.

Chapter Nine

It was almost noon when Kelly pulled up before Kim's chalet and parked the jeep. She hurried up to the door, key in hand. As if by magic, it opened before her. Brad, clad in a red turtleneck shirt and jeans, stood grinning down at her. His favorite blue twill baseball cap and parka and gloves were piled on the back of the chair. Beside it on the floor rested his dark blue backpack. He displayed none of the injured, woebegone air she'd expected him to assume when leaving.

With more confidence than she felt, Kelly said in brisk tones, "If I hadn't asked you to leave, I'd think you were setting out for an afternoon of skiing."

His grin broadened. "Right! I've been counting the hours till your return so you could go with me." He glanced at his watch. "You've been gone exactly two hours and twenty-two minutes, my love. I've been pacing the floor, worrying, wondering if the jeep broke down, if you'd had an accident, if someone ran into you . . ."

Suppressing a grin, Kelly said sternly, "I've told you, again and again, I'm fine. You've no right to worry about me!"

He gave her an engaging grin. "I know, but I worry anyway. It's my nature to worry about people I love."

"Okay, okay. But the things you worry about never happen."

He put an arm around her waist and drew her close against him. Placing his free hand under her chin, he forced her to look into his eyes. "What did happen?"

Kelly shook her head and, in spite of herself, felt grateful for his comforting arm around her. "Would you believe that maniac Smythe followed me from the police station? He must have seen the jeep parked outside. Maybe he thought I was Kim, I don't know. All I know is, on my way home, he tried to run me off the road."

"Good Lord, Kelly! How did you get away?"

Calmly, matter-of-factly, she told him. When she had finished, he went straight to the phone. "I'm reporting this to Captain Creel."

Kelly's lips curled in a skeptical smile. "He'll say I'm imagining things, that I'm unharmed, and that unless Smythe attacks me, he can do nothing."

As though she hadn't spoken, Brad leafed through Kim's phone book, found the number, and dialed. In strong no-nonsense tones he demanded to be put through to Captain Creel. Kelly sank down on the couch, listening to him tell Captain Creel her story, insisting the department provide police protection. Moments later he slammed down the phone, his handsome face contorted with anger and disgust.

"What did he say?"

Brad's voice was tight with annoyance. "He said you were nervous and upset over your sister being gone."

"And . . . ?"

"That you were probably imagining things — that unless the man attacks you, he can do nothing."

Kelly rolled her eyes heavenward. "I'm not going to say, 'I told you so.' "

"Well, that really tears it." He threw out his hands in a helpless gesture. "I'll have to stay here to protect you."

Kelly jumped up from the couch. "You'll do no such thing! I can take care of myself. Haven't I just proved it? Don't think you're going to use this — this little brush with that creep to con me into letting you stay here."

He let out a sigh of mock-resignation.

"Whatever's fair. I'm still going skiing. I hoped you'd go with me . . ."

"I'm not going skiing. I'm going to look for Kim."

"So am I, love. So am I. You told me that this man Smythe said Kim had gone on a cross-country tour. So — I called the lodge and talked to the tour director. She said there was a large group and she assumed, since Kim signed up for it, she'd gone, but she couldn't say for sure. She also checked with the ski patrol. They reported only one sprained ankle and two broken legs. No other accident victims in the past two weeks. She told me the trail the group had taken, and I'm going to check it out. Sorry you don't want to come along." He shrugged into his parka, slapped his hat on his head, and turned toward the door. "Oh, by the way, I have to pick up a few things at the ski shop: cross-country skis, bindings, boots, poles, map, compass. Mind if I borrow your car?"

Kelly took a deep breath to compose herself. Brad had bested her again, putting her in a no-win situation. When Kim was involved, she had no defense. "If you think you're going off to look for Kim without me, you're wrong!"

The corners of his mouth curved in an affable smile. "I *didn't* think of going without you — not for a minute!"

Gliding down the wide trail beside Brad, past dark evergreens laden with snow, Kelly felt the chill, bracing air sting her cheeks, and a feeling of exhilaration swept through her. It was like old times, skiing swiftly through the forest at Brad's side. She could be almost happy, she thought, if only the reason for their outing had been different.

She felt more encouraged when they passed a tall pine emblazoned with light blue three-inch enamel dots. "At least the trail is well marked!" said Kelly. "Even a novice like Kim could follow it."

Brad gave a doubtful shake of his head. "The tour director said it was a weekend outing, with forty-five miles of trails. Kim could easily have fallen behind and taken a wrong turn."

Kelly swallowed hard. In quavering tones she asked, "Do you think she's wandered around the mountain for days and finally fallen in a heap somewhere, lying frozen —"

Quickly Brad interrupted. "No, no, of course not. I think she'd have realized she took a wrong turn, and by the time she got back on the trail, the others were probably too far ahead for her to catch up. The director said everyone took a three-hour class in survival techniques, and I'm sure Kim is smart enough to use them. She also said everyone wore backpacks with emergency supplies." He shot her a confident grin. "And if Kim's anything like her sister — and she's identical — she can take care of herself."

Kelly felt briefly reassured. Kim *could* take care of herself. The backpack would explain why Kim's luggage, and what appeared to be all her clothes, were still stashed away in the closet. But it wouldn't explain why they hadn't heard from her, why she was still gone. Nor would it explain why her chalet had been broken into, or why a burglar would pass up a jewelry box — unless he was looking for something else! Had the intruder she'd surprised in the living room found what he was after? All she could think of that seemed to be missing were Kim's genealogy notes and, knowing Kim, she had probably taken her notes with her.

They pushed ahead in an easy rhythm, kick, stride, kick, stride, kick, stride, shouting Kim's name at frequent intervals, their voices reverberating in the silent forest. They had been under way for almost an hour when the sun retreated behind the clouds and big light dry snowflakes began drifting down in a desultory fashion. A soft gray pall crept across the virgin snow.

Kelly glanced up, scowling at the darkening sky. "Looks ominous," she said, feeling suddenly uneasy.

Brad grinned. "Relax. What's a little powder? Try to think of it as a perfect martini — very dry and sought after."

Kelly made no reply. She knew Brad was trying to cheer her, to keep up her spirits with his lighthearted banter, but all she could think of was this desperate, last-ditch search for Kim, so instead of relieving her anxiety, his amiable chatter annoyed her.

As if sensing her irritation, he said no more.

They followed a bridle path up an easy grade for almost four miles when they came to a "Y" intersection.

Brad pulled a map of the ski area from his pocket. "Which way? The cross-country tour headed north."

Kelly shook her head. "If Kim wanted to come down the mountain, she'd have turned downhill, wouldn't she?"

"But if she was trying to follow the tour group, she'd go with the marked trail. Right?"

Kelly gave a helpless shrug. "Your guess is as good as mine."

Brad stood frowning, considering. "Let's take the left fork a few hundred yards and see what's there. If it doesn't look promising, we'll backtrack and head north."

They pushed on, winding around the steep mountainside, twisting through aspen forests and stands of Douglas fir. Shortly they emerged in a clearing halfway up the side of one of the seven peaks of Blue Angel Mountain and came to a halt, gazing down at a sparsely forested slope that had evidently suffered a fire. They stood silent for a moment, admiring the magnificent view of the distant crags of the Gore Range to the west, then gazing east over the sprawling smoky-blue-colored chain of the Williams Fork Mountains, whose delicate tones blended into the white-crusted field patches of green and gray in the wide river valley below.

A dark shadow moving swiftly across the white landscape caught Kelly's eye. Looking up, she saw overhead a turkey buzzard soaring in lazy circles, as if honing in for a meal of carrion. A chill tingled down her spine. Perturbed, she turned to Brad, who had removed his sunglasses and was shrugging off the straps of his backpack. Swiftly he delved inside, pulled out a pair of field glasses, and peered through them, turning his head, sweeping back and forth across the vast snowy landscape. Without speaking, he handed her the binoculars.

She shoved her sun goggles over the top of her knitted cap and peered through the binoculars. Her heart pounded in her ears. Holding her breath, she scanned every inch of the terrain through a screen of softly falling snow. She let out her breath slowly. No small figure lay crumpled on the snow-clad slopes or had crashed into a tree trunk or slipped and fallen, caught in the folds of Blue Angel Mountain. She handed the glasses to Brad. "Let's move on."

Brad, who had been studying the map, said, "This trail loops around to the fork. We may as well forge ahead."

At the fork, the horse trail gave way to a hiking path, a steady, gentle climb. The spruce and aspen forest thinned, yielding to towering lodgepole pines.

Without warning, a raucous scream echoed through the silent woodland. Kelly let out a startled cry. There was a flapping of wings, and a flash of slate-blue feathers zoomed past her face, squawking loudly, as if scolding the intruders on its domain.

Brad laughed. "It's only a camp robber."

"A what?"

"Camp robber." Brad grinned. "A Canada jaybird."

"Oh." She managed a tremulous smile. "For a second it sounded like a human scream. I thought . . ."

Brad's expression changed to one of kindly concern. "I know what you thought, and you mustn't think such things. It's just as easy to think Kim is okay, and I'm sure she is. She's probably holed up somewhere waiting for someone to find her. She knows she could wear herself out wandering around lost, among a confusing web of look-alike ski trails and open areas. It's much more sensible for her to stay put."

Encouraged, reassured by Brad's optimistic outlook, Kelly tried to think positive thoughts. She pushed ugly words like *hypothermia, frostbite,* and *dehydration* far back in her mind. Of course they would find Kim, right as rain.

They had gone fewer than two miles when once again they emerged from the shelter of tall thick pines. The snow was falling heavier than she had realized. They halted at a weathered sign, **LEAN-TO**, pointing down a side trail. Brad pulled the map from his pocket and studied it, frowning.

"This trail leads to Rocky Falls lean-to. Then there's a steep ascent to Coyote Pass."

"Let's go for it!" With renewed vigor Kelly planted her poles and kicked out, Brad at her side. They skirted under the flank of Blue Angel Mountain on pillowy, rolling terrain, reveling in the swift, easy glide over fresh, soft powder. It would be perfect, a day to store in her memory forever — if only they could find Kim.

After a while the sky turned sullen and the dusky light that filtered through the clouds bathed the scene in somber, monochromatic shades of gray. Kelly and Brad gave up wiping their goggles dry and tucked them away in their pockets. The trail dipped abruptly into a bowl of white powder. Brad flew past her, following the fall line downhill. Kelly braked, then used her poles to keep her forward momentum on the gentle uphill slope. Thick swirling snowflakes stung her face, clung to her eyelids, obscuring her vision.

When at last the lean-to came into sight, Kelly's heart sank. It stood at the edge of an open area that had once been a lumberyard, a rough, three-walled, roofed hut with rude bunks to provide a nesting place for the skier in his sleeping bag. In front of the hut, the fast-falling snow covered the charred remains of a log fire that had once warmed ski tourers, now cold. Kelly turned to face Brad and blurted out what she'd been thinking. "Listen, Brad, I have this weird feeling we're not going to find Kim out here. I wish I hadn't let you talk me into this — this wild-goose chase. You yourself said she can take care of herself, and I agree. So let's go back to town. That's where the answer is, some-where in Blue Angel."

Brad eyed her for a moment without speaking, as if weighing his words. Finally he said, "All this time you and I have as-sumed Kim was gone because that was what she wanted. But suppose someone wanted her gone — and went along with her on the ski tour to make sure she didn't come back —"

Kelly gave a vigorous shake of her head, unwilling to believe anyone would harm Kim. "That doesn't make sense. Everyone wants her back: Eric, her boss Mr. Teague, the police *say* they're looking for her, and even the person who wrote that horrid note is waiting for her to come home. Please, Brad, let's go back to the chalet."

"There's one other place I want to check out. If she's not there, it's back to Blue Angel. Okay?"

Kelly nodded. "Let's go!"

Brad studied the map again, then looked up, scowling at the darkening sky. Folding the map and putting it away, he jerked his head toward a wide cut on the far side of the clearing. "That's an old logging road. The map shows a miner's cabin about two and a half miles up, where it dead-ends. Kim could be holed up there. Or would you rather push on to Coyote Pass?"

Kelly surveyed the narrow path, then eyed the logging road. "If Kim came this way, I think she'd opt for the road, especially if she had a map and knew at the end of it she'd find a cabin."

Brad nodded agreeably. "Right on!"

They set out across the snowy clearing.

Chapter Ten

The road swung east, then climbed slowly and steadily up the steep, rock-ribbed slope. Patches of pale green, gray, and brown lichen clung to rocks rising on either side of the road. All Kelly could hear was her own breathing in the thin, frosty air. Thank heaven her skiing weekends in Vermont had kept her in shape for cross-country skiing. A sudden loud thrashing in the woodland to her right shattered the silence. Kelly halted midstride, her heart hammering in her chest. The next moment a young doe with wild, frightened eyes crashed through the under-brush, dashed across the road, and vanished among the trees.

A slightly hysterical laugh escaped her. "Good Lord, that animal scared me!"

Brad halted beside her, grinning. "Just be thankful there are no snowmobiles tearing down the trail."

Ranks of tall, thin lodgepole pines gave way to spruce and alpine fir. The wind quickened and Kelly glanced up to see the branches thrashing in wide arcs above their heads. As they lunged on up the curling trail, the firs became dwarfed and gnarled, their limbs seeming to writhe in torture from the struggle to survive in their hostile environment.

Brad said, "We're above the timberline." He nodded toward a twisted, stunted evergreen. "I've read about them. They're called krummholz or wind timber." He slowed his pace to glide along beside her. "These storms seldom last long. In an hour the sun could be shining."

He didn't say what they both knew: that a storm brought with it a bigger danger: New snowfalls, even though they made for the most exciting skiing, also brought the greatest threat of avalanches.

At last the dim gray shape of the miner's cabin loomed up before them, veiled by the fine white curtain of falling snow. There was a forlorn, deserted air about it that made Kelly's heart turn over. No flickering light shone from the windows, no wisp of smoke curled from the chimney. Kim would have had no matches to start a fire, but she could still be inside, sleeping like the . . . *That* wouldn't bear thinking about. They halted before the door.

Brad gave a shout of laughter. "Look at this!"

Kelly smiled in spite of herself. In big, uneven block letters carved across the door were the words: **DO NOT DESTROY. HOOK DOOR WHEN LEAVING. LEAVE THINGS ALONE.**

Brad unhooked the door and shouted into the dusky cabin. "Hello! Anybody here?" Only the profound silence of snow falling at their backs answered his shout.

Kim *had* to be here! Quickly Kelly shed her skis and dashed inside, looking frantically around her. The place smelled of damp earth and wet charred wood. In the murky half-light coming through the doorway, she saw that the cabin was empty. She felt like bursting into tears. As Brad stamped inside after her, she said in tight, choked tones, "I knew Kim wouldn't be here!"

He flung an arm about her shoulders, giving her a comforting hug. "Well, now, this isn't the end of the world. She's got to be *some*where, and wherever she is, we'll find her. Maybe a little food will make things look brighter."

He swung his backpack to the floor, dug out a flashlight, and flicked the bright beam around the one-room cabin. The place was starkly bare. A shoulder-high shelf on one wall held a battered tin pan and a spoon, two moth-eaten army blankets, and a ragged patchwork quilt. Beside the fireplace on the far wall lay a small stack of pine knots apparently left by a previous occupant.

Brad set about building a fire. Kelly took down the patchwork quilt and spread it on the floor before the fireplace. Discouraged, depressed, she dropped down on the quilt, drew her knees up under her chin, and locked her arms around them, watching the bright yellow tongues of flame. The smell of pine pervaded the room. The fire took hold, driving away the chill. The glow from the leaping flames highlighted the angular planes of Brad's cheekbones, his full warm mouth, his strong stubborn chin. At the moment he looked so endearing that her traitorous heart turned over.

Brad hunkered down beside her. From his backpack he fished out several packs of cheese and peanut butter crackers, two thick submarine sandwiches, two chocolate bars, two cups, and a handful of tea bags.

Almost accusingly she said, "You knew we wouldn't find Kim, didn't you! That it would be a long search. That's why you brought food along."

Brad shot her a lopsided smile. "Not at all. When we find Kim, she may be hungry.

Besides, when I hit the wilderness trail, I believe in being well armed — like making a presentation to a client, I go well prepared. I picked up this stuff at the cafeteria while you were getting your gear."

"I see," she said quietly. Summoning a smile, she said, "I'm glad you did. I'm starving!"

They shed their parkas and boots, and, basking in the warmth of the bright, cheerful fire, devoured their food. Downing the last of her chocolate bar, Kelly said, thinking aloud, "You know, I wonder if Kim's digging around could have unearthed some family skeletons that someone in town doesn't want brought to light? Even the police would try to protect the old-timers. And that someone might have good reason to want her gone."

"Gone, maybe," said Brad quickly, "but not dead."

"No," agreed Kelly, "not that! I'm trying to think what else Kim might have done that would get her in trouble."

"Well, she is an accountant, and a damned good one. But that should keep her out of trouble."

Kelly sat bolt upright. "Not necessarily. Suppose, while she was keeping Alpenstock's accounts, she found that someone was fiddling with the books?"

Brad's eyes lighted with interest. "Corporate theft? A good possibility. Proving it is something else."

"Just watch me! I can hardly wait to get back to town to stir things up. I think I'll start with Mr. Teague!" Brad made no reply, but gathered up the wrappers from their food and tossed them in the fire. Kelly slipped into her parka and reached for her boots. "Let's move on out."

Brad glanced up at the window. A worried scowl furrowed his brow. Following his gaze, Kelly let out a gasp of astonishment. "It's pitch dark!"

Brad nodded. "The sun sinks over the yardarm real fast out here behind these mountain peaks."

Kelly sprang to her feet and threw open the door, letting in a bitter cold blast of air. Although it had almost stopped snowing, the yawning darkness seemed to hold her at bay. She slammed the door shut and wheeled to face Brad.

"Keep your flashlight out, we're going to need it."

Slowly Brad unfolded his long lanky body from the quilt and stood up. He strode to the door, opened it a crack, and peered out. Gently he closed the door and stood leaning his back against it.

"Listen, Kelly, it's black as the hole of Calcutta out there. The flash won't give us enough light — and you never know when it'll conk out. We'll have to wait till morning."

Kelly's lips thinned in a stubborn line. Here it comes, she thought, the soft sell. "Okay," she said agreeably. "*You* wait till morning. *I'm* heading out."

His eyes darkened and his voice had a sharp edge to it. "It would be crazy to start out now. It's not only dark, it's freezing cold."

Kelly felt heat rising inside her that had nothing to do with the blazing fire.

Brad captured her wrists in a strong grip and pulled her to him, holding her tightly against his chest. His dark deep-set eyes, reflecting golden sparks of firelight, seemed to burn into her. "Be sensible, Kelly. I'm sure wherever Kim is, she's safe and sound."

Kelly let out a hysterical laugh. "You're *sure* she's safe and sound! Well, I *know!* I'm her twin. Call it ESP or intuition, or coincidence, I know she's in trouble! She needs me!" She burst into tears.

Brad curved an arm snugly about her waist. Smoothing her hair, pressing her head close to his chest, he said in soft, cajoling tones, "Take another look, my love.

Maybe you'll believe what I'm saying." He opened the door.

Kelly peered around his shoulder. The soft, silent powder was falling again, thick and fast. If anything, the storm had worsened, and showed no sign of letting up. Wearily she pushed the door to, and leaned her head against it. Through her closed lids, tears trickled down her cheeks. She heard Brad moving about the cabin, and the next moment felt his hands on her shoulders turning her to face him.

He crooked a finger under her chin, tilting her face up to his. He bent his head and kissed her eyelids, kissed away the tears on her cheeks, kissed the dimple in her chin. Refusing to be consoled, she turned her head away, before his warm, loving lips touched her own. He placed firm, gentle hands on her cheeks, forcing her to look up into his face. His eyes held hers, mirroring such tenderness and compassion that she wanted to cry out.

"Listen, Kelly, I have my intuitions, too. *I* think Kim is every bit as sensible as you are. You two are on the same wavelength, right?" Wordlessly Kelly nodded. "You're smart enough to save yourself, and so is Kim. You have to have faith in her, faith in someone other than yourself. You can't worry about all the things that *might* happen, or you'll be climbing the walls, and that won't help Kim worth a damn." He put an arm about her shoulders and his voice took on a commanding tone. "Come sit by the fire and keep warm. We'll get a good night's sleep and tomorrow we'll start out fresh."

She let him lead her across the cabin where he'd spread the army blankets over the quilt. She looked down, frowning. "Why can't we each roll up in a blanket?"

He grinned down at her. "It's warmer this way. Save energy, share a blanket. Much warmer than sleeping single. Just snuggle down inside and you'll be warmer than a butterfly in a cocoon."

Kelly laughed. "A butterfly isn't a butterfly till it hatches! Before then it's just a plain old pupa — a sleeping caterpillar!"

He shook his head in mock despair. "Sorry, sweetie, you'll never pass for a caterpillar." His admiring gaze traveled over her slender body. "You haven't the figure for it." He gave her a swat on the bottom. "Crawl in the sack. In the morning you'll feel like flying."

There was no use arguing with him. If she had to give in, she might as well put a good face on it. A spark of amusement lighted her soft brown eyes. "Brad, you're impossible."

"With me all things are possible. Give me your parka."

In silent surrender she slipped off her pink parka. Brad spread it on top of the blanket along with his own. She slid under the blankets and lay flat on her stomach, her chin resting on her folded arms, gazing moodily into the fire. Brad slid in beside her, also on his stomach, propped on his elbows, gazing dreamily into the fire.

He let out a long, contented sigh. "Like old times, isn't it, my love, stretching out before the fire, dreaming dreams."

Little warning prickles tinged through her. Without looking at him, she said in low, even tones, "Brad, this is *not* like old times, and I am *not* your love! I wish you'd remember that."

He gave a hopeless shake of his head. "It's hard to remember — uphill all the way."

Avoiding his gaze, she stared at the bright blue and yellow flames leaping up the chimney. "You have to try, Brad. You're not trying, flying out here, tracking me down . . ."

"I am trying!" He sighed deeply. "It just isn't working out."

"You'll have to try harder."

He feigned an injured air. "Look, Kelly, I'm not some rent-a-car company, I'm a human being!"

She started to say, What you are is a walking menace, a threat to the heart and soul of every female you meet, but at once thought better of it. She made no reply but stared fixedly into the fire crackling on the hearth.

He bent his head to peer into her face, as if to assure himself that she was still awake. With one finger he traced the curve of her ear. Softly he said, "I'm a human being, and you're a human being, not one of your machines at Conover Executive Suites."

Though she refused to listen to what he was saying, the touch of his finger stroking her ear was disconcerting. She brushed his hand away as she would a mosquito and turned her face to him.

"Brad, I want to have a serious talk with you. I —"

His full, generous mouth split in a wide grin. "Good. It's about time we got serious."

Her lips thinned in an exasperated line. "I've been serious all along. Now I'm telling you, once and for all, being independent, starting my own business is a lifelong dream. I have to prove to myself I can make a success of it. I have no time, no place in my life for a husband." Struck by a thought, she said, "It's like what you just said — I want to *fly!*"

Softly he said, "There's more than one way to fly — more than one airline — more than one place to go." His fingers trailed along the back of her neck, tracing the delicate curve of her other ear.

She brushed his hand away. In forceful tones she said, "I have one goal, to make a success of Executive Suites, and everything I do is geared toward that goal." She looked him squarely in the eyes and struck what she intended to be the final blow. "We are not meant for each other. When two people are *really* meant for each other, they both agree that they are. So if I say we're not, we're not. Got it?"

A sober, serious expression shone from his fine dark eyes. "Got it. At last I see where you're coming from. You're absolutely right. You have to devote every waking — and sleeping — moment to Executive Suites." His voice rang with enthusiasm. "I totally approve and admire a person with singleness of purpose. It's the only way to succeed. So this is good-bye. Right?"

"Right!"

Brad eased from under the blankets and stood up, glancing around the dark-shadowed corners of the cabin. "Now where did I put my boots?"

"Your boots!" exclaimed Kelly. "Are your feet cold?"

Vigorously he shook his head. He stared up at the ceiling with the martyred air of a saint burning at the stake. "I'm going. I know when I'm not wanted. I'm off, out into the storm."

"You idiot! You can't go now!"

His face brightened, his dark curling brows rising several notches. "I can't?"

With some asperity Kelly said, "You know perfectly well you can't. Haven't you just finished telling me how foolhardy it would be to go out in this storm? Crawl back in the sack — and go to sleep!"

Watching him over her shoulder, she thought she saw the corners of his lips quirk in a faint, triumphant smile. He eased down beside her. She pillowed her head on her arms and pulled the blankets up over her head. She would simply ignore him and go to sleep. But an uneasy thought lurking just out of reach in the back of her mind defied sleep. Finally it came to her. He had given in too easily. He was far too agreeable — not at all like the aggressive Brad York she knew so well.

All at once she let out an astonished yelp. Something cold and hard and wiggly was pressing against her calves. She raised her head, looking at Brad in the flickering fire-light. His eyes were closed, his thick dark lashes shadowing his high cheekbones, his face a mask of peaceful innocence.

"Brad York, keep your feet to yourself!"

Drowsily he murmured, "They're cold."

Kelly felt his legs move upward, sliding over her calves, her thighs, her bottom. Swiftly she rolled over. Reaching down under the scratchy army blanket, she groped for the legs now sprawled across her hips. She grabbed hold of a hairy muscular shin and heaved it off her stomach. "Keep your feet to yourself and go to sleep."

Brad's eyes remained tightly closed. "I'm trying to, but you're causing so much com-motion I can't."

"You're the one causing the commotion. Move your other leg over on your side."

"Don't get upset, my love." As though un-aware that she had rolled over, he reached out a hand as if to give her a comforting pat on the back and patted her left breast in-stead. Gently, fondly, he patted it again. A delicious thrill surged through her. Her breasts seemed to swell, her nipples hard-ening into peaks of desire.

Through gritted teeth she almost shouted, "Brad, move!"

She felt the weight of his leg lift from her

hips, and his knee, moving in slow, sensuous motions across her stomach, slid down the dark valley between her thighs, parting her legs. His warm, gentle hand curved around her other breast, caressing the tip with thumb and forefinger.

"Brad!" She clutched his arm and flung it from her.

"Now, don't get excited, my love."

"Excited!" she shouted. "Who's excited! And I'm not your love!"

He let out a resigned sigh. "Okay, you're not my love."

His words fell like stones on her ears. Perversely, hearing him say she was not his love was both unpleasant and unsettling. She clamped her lips shut and glared at the firelight dancing on the ceiling.

Brad rolled over on his side, and propped on one elbow, stared down into her face. "You forgot to kiss me good-night. We always kiss good-night, remember?"

She didn't want to remember. Remembering was far too dangerous. Faster than light, his free hand clasped the back of her head. His lips, hard and compelling, moved over hers. She put her hands on his shoulders and pushed him away.

"I kissed you good-night. Now go to sleep!"

Grinning down at her, he clasped both her hands in his and brought them to his lips. "That was good-night. Now a kiss for good-bye."

He bent his head to hers. Quickly she jerked her head aside. His lips nuzzled her ear. A shiver that had nothing to do with the chill in the cabin tingled down her spine. Softly, persuasively, he whispered, "You owe me that, Kelly. Kiss your lover good-bye."

Unaccountably, mist stung her eyes. She turned her face toward him, and his lips, warm and seeking, claimed hers. When she thought she could endure the joy of it no longer, she drew back, her eyes closed, breathless, longing for love. She wanted to say, That was good-bye, Brad, but the words stuck in her throat. He kissed her eyelids. She could feel his breath warm on her cheek. His lips brushed hers. "And now, my love, one more kiss for the road."

His lips parted hers, his tongue seeking, exploring. Her knees seemed to melt like tallow. Sternly she told herself she was weak-willed and spineless with no more resistance than a candle in the wind. A small voice inside her head said, *Right!* Her arms stole around his neck and she clung to him as if there were no tomorrow.

A pine knot disintegrated, sending a fountain of sparks up the chimney. Brad raised his head for a fraction of a second, as if to make certain no sparks strayed, then bent his head to hers, whispering, "Since Christmas is coming, and I won't be here, this is for Christmas."

An ecstatic sigh escaped her. How could she deny Brad York a Christmas present? Eagerly she responded with her lips, her hands, stroking his thick curling hair, stroking the back of his neck. The cabin had suddenly become very warm. She unbuttoned Brad's flannel shirt. He unbuttoned hers. Her hands slid up under his tee-shirt, her fingers trailing over his warm, furred chest. His hands crept upward, under her turtleneck sweater. Somehow his legs became entwined with hers. She willed her legs to move, but they refused to do her bidding.

Slowly he raised his head, and drew back from her, gazing searchingly into her face. She could not tell whether the small fires that burned in his eyes were reflected firelight, or something much deeper. His lips curved in a radiant smile.

"That was the greatest Christmas present ever!"

Softly she murmured, "What about your birthday?"

"Oh Lord, yes! How could I forget my

birthday! You always give me a present on my birthday." Swiftly his mouth covered hers. She locked her arms about his waist, hugging him close, closer, ever closer. By the time they had done Valentine's Day, Easter, the Fourth of July, Halloween, and Thanksgiving, the cabin had grown unbearably warm.

"Here," Brad said, "you don't need this heavy sweater." With one swift motion he stripped it up over her head and tossed it away.

"And you don't need this tee-shirt!" said Kelly, sliding it up over his head and tossing it away.

Laughing, giggling, taking turns, they flung off each other's clothes, one by one, until they all lay in a heap atop the blankets.

"Kelly, my love," said Brad in low, seductive tones, "we're going to make this a night to remember!"

In a spirit of joyous abandon, Brad rolled onto his back, locked his arms about her slender waist, and rolled her over on top of him, clasping her tightly against his broad, muscular chest.

Feigning indignation, Kelly shrieked, "Brad, you know I can't stand to be held down!"

His arms tightened about her waist.

167

Laughing, he said, "Try to think of us as one, with me as your better half."

"Ha!" scoffed Kelly, grinning down at him. "You must be the most arrogant man in the world! Besides, I was born with another half — Kim!" Struggling to free herself from his grasp, she kicked out, her feet colliding with Brad's hairy shins. Swiftly she slid her hands down his sides, found his ribs, and dug in her fingers, tickling his hard, taut muscles.

With a howl of mock pain, dark eyes sparkling with devilment, Brad caught both her wrists in one hand, holding them in a strong grip under his chin, and clapped his free hand across her bare bottom.

Fused to Brad, hip to hip, Kelly let out a shriek and, feet thrashing, writhed against his warm, lean body.

She heard his sharp intake of breath, felt his legs move under her, evading her flailing feet, so that they thudded harmlessly on the thick quilt.

Huskily he said, "If you're nice, I'll let you be my better half."

Gasping, laughing, she murmured, "Thanks, but no thanks."

He released her hands and trailed his fingers up the side of her cheek, around the curve of her ear, stroking the back of her neck, toying with wisps of golden hair. Softly, persuasively, he said, "We'd make a great team, you and I."

She raised up on her elbows and smiled down into his face. The flickering firelight accentuated his dark deep-set eyes, highlighted the planes of his cheekbones, his wide full lips and strong jaw. In his eyes she saw a yearning so tender, so intense, it seemed to consume her. A small stab of guilt shot through her. It was wrong to encourage him when she knew they had no future together. Lightly she said, "We make a good team, I never denied that — but, as someone once said, Kipling, maybe, 'He travels the fastest who travels alone.' That's *my* motto!"

Brad gazed up into her face, regarding her in silent appraisal. The look of a wounded animal in his eyes wrenched at her heart. Unable to endure his anguished gaze, she braced her hands on the quilt and rose up as if to leave him.

She felt the touch of his warm hands on her shoulders, holding her lightly. He raised his head, his lips caressing the soft valley between her breasts. She bent her head to his, strewing gentle kisses over the top of his thick, unruly black hair. He nuzzled her breasts, igniting small sparks of desire within her. His lips traveled upward, lingering at the hollow in her throat, trailing up the gentle curve of her neck, nibbling her earlobe. His mouth brushed her lips, her cheeks, her eyelids. A warning voice inside her head protested. *It isn't fair to lead him on!* The warning went unheeded as his lips closed over hers. His arms went around her, drawing her close against him. Her knees felt weak, her feet sought his, sliding down the length of his lean, muscular legs. Somewhere in the back of her mind passed the fleeting thought that she must give him a night to remember. She curved her arms about his neck in a fervent embrace, responding to his kisses with a passion that only inflamed him further. Through half-lidded eyes she saw a look of rapture suffusing his rugged features. His shoulders, gleaming with a sheen of perspiration, glowed golden in the firelight. Their passion mounted in an explosion of joy, their bodies melding in an embrace that Kelly wished would never end.

Lying in dreamy contentment in Brad's arms, she felt a sense of euphoria steal over her. For a few ecstatic moments, Brad had made her forget that Kim was gone. Even now, a feeling of happiness flowed through her. She felt complete, as though all were right with her world. Smiling to herself, she thought this was truly a night to remember, though a bittersweet memory it may be. With a small stab of nostalgia, as if she'd already lost something precious, she thought wistfully that making love was a fitting end to their relationship — so much more pleasant than a heartrending scene — to quench the fires of their passions in a blaze of glory. Tomorrow Brad would go away, out of her life forever. Suddenly, she did not want to think about tomorrow.

Chapter Eleven

Kelly awoke the next morning cross as a bear. She had overslept, when what she really wanted to do was to keep looking for Kim. When she got back to town, she would try to track down the reason for Kim's disappearance. If only she could find out *why* Kim was gone, maybe she could find out *where* she'd gone!

She glanced over at Brad, the smile on his sleeping face reminding her of a wolf who had devoured a rabbit. Glaring at him, she told herself, "That's what you are, Kelly Conover, a rabbit! You've no more sense than a rabbit, falling for his line about making this a night to remember." He'd said he was leaving, and then he'd taken advantage of her. Making love to her, holding her captive in this blasted blanket roll. Furious with him, she was even more furious with herself for letting him seduce her half the night and causing her to oversleep.

She sat up abruptly. The fire had gone

out, and a bitter cold blast of air enveloped her. Now here she was, naked as a jaybird, shivering to death. She grabbed her clothes, slid down under the covers, and began pulling them on. She stuck out a foot and gave Brad a sharp kick in the shins.

"Brad, wake up! Here you are, lolling in bed, and the morning's half gone!"

He opened one eye. "Aren't *you* lolling in bed?"

"No," she snapped. "I'm getting dressed, and I wish you'd do the same."

He opened both eyes, and through narrowed lids gazed at the pearly half-light sifting through the window. He glanced at his watch, scowling.

"The morning's half gone, all right. It's quarter of seven." He yawned widely and curved an arm about her waist, pulling her toward him. "Baby, it's cold outside. We'd better warm up a little before we head out."

Kelly, arms behind her, hooking her bra, jerked away. Briskly she said, "Put your clothes on, if you want to be warm. And if you're going with me you'd better hurry, because I'm going now!"

Brad groaned and reached for his clothes. "You're a drivin' woman, my love. Enough to drive a man to distraction." He shot her a disarming smile. "But don't worry, I won't let you drive alone."

Holding on to her patience by a thread, she said in low even tones, "I am not worried about me, I'm worried about Kim."

She finished dressing, got to her feet, combed her fingers through her hair, and donned her parka and scarf. By the time she finished pulling on her boots, Brad was up and dressed, whistling his favorite song "Just Hanging Around." She gritted her teeth and said nothing.

They emerged from the cabin into a silent white world. Deep, feathery powder, unpacked, untouched, untracked, perfect for deep powder skiing, spread out before them. All at once Kelly's heart contracted. From the corner of her eye she saw a grotesque frozen figure that appeared to be writhing in pain. Startled, she cried out, "What's that?"

"Snow ghosts," said Brad with unfailing good humor.

Blinking at the apparition in the sunlight, she let out a small relieved sigh. Just for a moment, the heavy snow clinging to the sparse, weather-beaten pines had looked like a small frozen figure.

They skied swiftly, smoothly, back down the logging trail. The morning sun, rising behind the mountain peaks, tinted the sparkling snowy slopes with a golden rosy glow as they flew down the road, reveling in the sparkling pure air, the deep untracked powder, the long smooth descent.

At the fork they turned west and, following Brad's map, crossed a snowmobile trail, dropped into a small valley, then began a gentle climb. They crossed a low pass and entered an open glade and skied between the trees. Ignoring the well-traveled routes dotted with early-bird skiers, they looped around the more remote trails, unplowed roads, hiking trails, and bridle paths. Again and again they shouted Kim's name. With each passing hour the high hopes that had buoyed Kelly in the early morning dimmed. By four-thirty in the afternoon, they had covered the entire network of trails. There was no trace of Kim. Kelly felt as though her world had stopped turning.

As they drove back to Blue Angel a pall of discouraged silence enveloped them, ironically uniting them in gloom if not in love, thought Kelly dully. Brad pulled up before the chalet, reached across her, and opened the door.

"I'll let you out here, sweetie. I'm going to park the jeep around back, then check out the plane." He shot her a facetious grin. "Have to make sure none of the Blue Angels made off with it while we were gone."

Kelly grinned back. "Call me if you need any help." She slid from the jeep and started up the walk, digging in her purse for her house key. As Brad roared away down the road the cold gray twilight seemed to close in around her. She wished he'd come to the door with her instead of going to check his plane. It was hard to see the lock in the gathering dusk. She bent down, jammed the key in the frozen lock, twisted the knob, and threw open the door.

She stepped inside the dim, gloomy chalet and stopped stock-still, paralyzed with shock. She heard her own terrified voice cry out, "Oh no!" The same moment she sensed rather than saw a tall shadowy figure lunge from behind the open door, felt a sharp blow at the base of her skull, then sank into darkness.

She awoke in Brad's arms as he started carrying her up the stairs. "Brad, I'm fine, really! put me down."

"Sure?" Worried concern shone from his dark eyes as he set her gently on her feet.

"I'm sure." Gingerly she felt the back of her head. "Just a little headache." She turned to survey the room. "This is what really gives me a headache!"

Once again every desk drawer was pulled out, upended, the contents dumped on the floor. All Kim's books were swept from the shelves in a heap beside them. Couch and chair cushions were strewn about the room. She glanced down the hall. The closet door stood open, Kim's belongings spilled out into the hallway.

She flung out her arms in a hopeless gesture. "Why? Why do these people keep coming back, harassing me?"

Brad scowled. "I can only think of one reason, Kelly, and it's not very pleasant. Someone around here thinks Kim has come back — and brought with her something they want."

Angry color crept up Kelly's cheeks into her hairline. Venomously she said, "I'll bet it was that creep Smythe looking for whatever it is he thinks Kim stole."

"And if he doesn't find it, he's going to play rough. You've got to watch every step, Kelly. Always on guard."

"How can I, when he can walk in here any time of day or night? What really bothers me is how he gets in!"

"Same way I did, I imagine," said Brad with a helpless shake of his head. "Slides a credit card past the lock."

Suddenly she felt terribly threatened, almost violated by this unknown intruder who had ravaged Kim's house.

Brad put an arm around her shoulders, hugging her close to his side. "Look, Kelly, I know you think Kim found out something — about someone's past in Blue Angel or some fiddling with the accounts at Alpenstock — and that Smythe is behind all this. So okay, Smythe is suspect A. But maybe it wasn't Smythe. Maybe there's suspect B. Just a plain old everyday burglar — looking for money or jewelry."

"Jewelry!" Kelly exclaimed. She ducked from under Brad's consoling arm and raced upstairs to the loft. Kim's bedside lamp was on, and in its gleam she saw what she had expected to see. The room was a shambles. The spread and blanket had been flung from the bed, the mattress thrown on the floor. The dresser and armoire had been rifled, drawers turned upside down, inside out, clothes strewn everywhere.

Quickly she crossed to the dresser. Kim's petit point–covered jewelry box had been pried open, the contents dumped in a heap on the top. There lay her grandmother's gold bracelet, her mother's marquisette brooch, a strand of pearls she'd given Kim on her birthday. Obviously robbery wasn't the motive, unless Kim had acquired something of value she hadn't told Kelly about — and that was highly unlikely.

Her gaze was caught by a small blue leather journal lying amid the heap of jewelry. Curious, she picked it up. On the cover in gold script was the single word: **TRAVELS**. Though reluctant to read Kim's private thoughts, she forced herself to leaf through it on the chance that Kim might have noted down something, anything, about a trip she had planned to take.

As she expected, each entry was dated and bore Kim's impression of places she'd seen in and around Blue Angel. With shaking fingers she flipped to the last entry and let out a hopeless sigh. The red bird Kim had been wooing would now fly to the kitchen window to peck at the sunflower seeds scattered on the sill. Kelly paged back through the journal and found other similar entries, until she came to November 22. There Kim had sketched a rough family tree starting with their parents, John and Mary Conover. Hastily she glanced over the names: Conovers had spouses named Byers, Ogilve, Hill, and Moffat. In cramped letters, squeezed on the bottom of the page, Kim had written: *County Court House*. Kelly finished leafing through the journal, to the last entry on

December 3. There was no mention of a trip.

With a sense of mingled disappointment and gloom, Kelly put the journal back in the box, heaped the jewelry on top, and closed the lid. Glancing over the loft railing, she saw Brad dialing the phone, heard him ask for Captain Creel. If there was one good thing about the break-in, she thought grimly, it was that it might at last convince the captain that there was something going on around here that would bear investigating.

Within the hour Sergeant Gilmer, looking very official and protective, with the air of a white knight rescuing a lady in distress, stepped inside the door. Smiling admiringly at Kelly, he looked slightly crestfallen when she introduced him to Brad York.

He stood clutching a clipboard under one arm, surveying the wreckage of the room with a sense of wonder, the fingers of his free hand stroking his blossoming moustache. Kelly wondered if he'd ever investigated a break-in before. He let out a deep sigh, took a pen from his pocket, braced the clipboard against his chest, and began filling out a form. "Name and address?"

Kelly groaned inwardly, wishing he could figure out something for himself. She gave him her name, address, approximate time and place of entry, and other pertinent information.

Pen poised over his clipboard, Sergeant Gilmer asked, "Now what did this guy look like?"

Annoyed with herself because she could give him no better answer, Kelly snapped. "I have no idea — only the impression that he was a man, someone taller than I am."

The sergeant appeared stunned. "You've got to be kidding!"

Barely controlling her temper, Kelly said, "It was dusk when we got home, dark as a cave in the chalet. When I opened the door and stepped inside, he was hiding *behind* the door. He let go a chop on the back of my head and I was out cold — and then he took off."

"Got it!" said Sergeant Gilmer. "Assailant unknown."

The stocky sergeant then made the rounds of the chalet. "No sign of forced entry," he remarked in disappointed tones. Brad stated his credit card theory and the sergeant nodded in quick agreement. Glancing at the drawers overturned on the living room floor, he said, "Couldn't have been a professional burglar. Pros pull out the drawers partway, starting with the lower drawer, sort through it, pull out the next, on up to the top. Saves time, you see."

"I see," said Kelly, trying to hide her exasperation. "But as far as I can tell, nothing is missing."

"Oh?" said Sergeant Gilmer, brightening. "That's a lucky break."

Kelly had the feeling that the sergeant was taking the whole thing with a grain of salt. If only she could have described her attacker!

"Break-ins are not lucky," said Brad sternly.

Sergeant Gilmer reddened. "Yes, I mean, no. But it's good that nothing was taken. There have been several robberies —"

Kelly interrupted. "What about fingerprints?"

The sergeant ran a befuddled hand over his smooth, shiny black hair. "It's hard to get a clear print, mucked up with all the others, you see. Besides, burglars usually wear gloves. And since nothing was stolen . . ."

Kelly could feel her temper rise. "And since nothing was stolen," she said hotly, "and robbery wasn't the motive, obviously there's another reason — one connected with Kim's disappearance. I hope you can convince Captain Creel that . . ."

The sergeant smiled apologetically. "Not

necessarily, Miss Conover. I'm sorry to say we get a number of reports of vandalism. Many of these places are vacant a lot of the time and vandals break in, looking for a little excitement. I'm sure Captain Creel will agree with me that this has nothing to do with your sister." He gave her a reassuring smile. "I'm sure she'll turn up soon. Just relax, Miss Conover." He cast an envious glance at Brad. "Enjoy your stay in Blue Angel." He tucked his clipboard under his arm and left.

Scowling, Kelly said, "He was no help at all!"

Brad flung an arm about her shoulders in a comforting hug. "I'm afraid the sergeant has done all he can do at the moment. He could be right. Kim could turn up any time." He gazed about the jumbled room. "Meanwhile I may as well make myself useful." He bent down, picked up a cushion, and set it on the couch.

In resigned silence Kelly set to helping Brad straighten the room. She was sliding a drawer back in the desk when she was startled from her dour thoughts by the shrill ringing of the phone. She lunged for it, sweeping the receiver to her ear. Brad stood watching her as though trying to read her reaction. Her face reflected disappointment, followed by surprise as Eric's smooth, accented tones came over the line.

Kelly brightened. "Yes, yes, of course." Her brows rose. "Can't you tell me now?" A short silence. "I understand. No, I don't mind. I'll meet you there at seven."

She put down the receiver and smiled at Brad. "That was Eric Brunner."

Brad's brows drew together, his chin jutted forward. "Oh? Who's Eric Brunner?"

"He's Kim's ski instructor."

"What's he want?"

"I'm trying to tell you. He's invited me out to dinner. Says he has something to tell me." Her eyes lighted with anticipation. "Maybe he's had news of Kim."

Coldly, Brad snapped, "That's a dumb idea. If he had news of Kim, he'd be really upset because he thinks you *are* Kim. So there's no need for you to go."

Defiantly she said, "I want to go. I want to hear whatever it is he has to say."

"Listen, you don't know this guy from the abominable snowman. If he's on the up and up, why couldn't he tell you over the phone?"

"He says it's personal. Doesn't want to discuss it over the phone."

Brad let out something like a snort. "Oh,

I'll bet! What he wants is to make time with you."

Struck with an inspiration, Kelly snapped, "What's wrong with that? I *like* Eric Brunner, and apparently he likes me." Maybe dating someone else would convince Brad once and for all that she didn't want to be tied down.

"Oh yeah? Well, in that case, I'd better go along to check this guy —"

"In a pig's eye you'll go along! I'm meeting him in the dining room at the lodge at seven — alone."

Brad planted his fists on his hips and glared down at her. "What kind of a guy would ask a girl to *meet* him someplace? Is he too lazy to come and pick you up? Or is he one of these ski bums who doesn't want a real job, just drifts from resort to resort, preying on innocent women and children? Or maybe he has no wheels! Doesn't he know these roads can be dangerous at night? I'm not going to let you —"

"Not *let* me!" Kelly turned on him with a wicked gleam in her eye and a disarming grin. "Those are fightin' words!"

His smile challenged her own. "Look, Kelly, you've just been knocked out. It would be much better if you stayed home and went to bed — with me, of course."

Kelly laughed. "Better for whom, my friend? No way you're going to take charge of my life again. I'm going to take a shower. Why don't you cool down with a can of Coors?" Lifting her chin in a defiant tilt, she sailed down the hall into the bathroom and slammed the door.

She had finished lathering her skin with Kim's jasmine-scented soap and was rinsing off when she heard a violent pounding on the shower door. Her heart stopped. Maybe Kim had called. Maybe she was on the phone. Maybe she was here! She slid the door open and let out an outraged gasp. Shrouded in a veil of steam, like a god descending from the clouds, stood Brad, nude except for a towel draped around his lean hips, an expectant smile on his lips. Beaming with good-humored cheer, he said, "I brought my own Safeguard soap. When's your lease up?"

"When I finish rinsing off!" said Kelly indignantly. "What do you mean, bursting in here?"

"I mean to take a shower, and I'm afraid the hot water will run out." His grin widened. "Haven't you heard my current slogan? Save water, share a shower!" He shoved back the shower door and stepped inside.

"You get out of here!" she shrieked, turning her back on him. She knew Brad York, knew only too well why he was invading her shower. Before she could say good-bye, drop dead, or kiss me, he'd be making love to her, making sure she'd miss her date with Eric.

As if she hadn't spoken, he went on. "Besides, you need me to soap your back." Briskly he rubbed the bar of soap across her gleaming wet shoulders, across her shoulder blades, down her slender spine. "Good grief, you're skinnier than an aspen." She felt a friendly pinch on her bottom. "You ought to get some meat on your bones. Now, if you go out to dinner with *me*, I'll —"

Kelly let out an outraged howl and plunged from the hot steamy shower. slamming the door shut after her. She snatched up a towel, wrapped it around her, and fled from the bathroom. All the way up the stairs to the loft she heard Brad's howls of laughter echoing after her.

He was impossible. Absolutely impossible! And incorrigible as well! How could she ever have actually admired his ambition, his resourcefulness, his originality, his business acumen, his determination to land every account he went after? How could she ever have thought he was the most clever, amusing, charming, fascinating man she'd ever met? He was so arrogant, domineering, and, yes, pigheaded, even if he was the handsomest man she'd ever met. She had to stop thinking about Brad York and consider what she'd wear tonight. She crossed to the armoire and flung open the door.

She reached for her favorite French blue ultrasuede skirt, and immediately thought better of it. Eric thought she was Kim. She could keep up the pretense much more effectively if she dressed in Kim's clothes.

Moments later she stood before the mirror over the dresser gazing critically at her reflection. An eerie feeling came over her, as if she were looking at Kim in her pale, peach-colored cashmere sweater and light brown- white- and peach-flecked tweed skirt. She opened Kim's jewelry box, took out her pearls, and fastened them around her neck. She could hear the water drumming in the shower downstairs and, above it, Brad singing loudly and slightly off-key, something about hanging around, hoping somebody would feel lonely and miss him.

Blast him! He knew how to get to a girl. She'd better slip out before he thought up some other scheme to keep her here. Luckily Kim seldom wore makeup, for there was no time to spare to do her face. She snatched up a bottle of Kim's perfume and sprayed a whiff behind each ear — a musky, woodsy scent, a reminder of Kim that made her heart ache.

She ran downstairs and dived into the closet. There was no romantic song echoing from the shower now. Brad must be toweling off. She flung Kim's black fake fur jacket over her arm, dashed to the front door, and let herself out, closing the door softly after her.

Chapter Twelve

"So you see," said Eric Brunner, unsmiling, watching Kelly with steady, penetrating blue eyes, "I think we've played your game long enough."

Kelly felt the color drain from her face. Caught off base, she sat staring at him, trying frantically to think what to say. They were seated at a table for four, Eric on her right, awaiting her explanation. Candles in wrought-iron chandeliers shed a soft glow over the white-clothed tables in the elegant, red-carpeted dining room at the lodge. Disconcerted, she shifted her gaze to the arrangement of pink carnations in the center of the table.

When she made no reply, Eric went on calmly, quietly, coldly polite, his slight Austrian accent emphasizing his deadly serious tone. He leaned toward her, staring directly into her eyes, his own eyes diamond hard.

"I don't like playing games when I don't know the rules, the purpose of the game, or the stakes. I'm extremely fond of Kim and terribly concerned for her safety. I asked you to meet me tonight, hoping you would appear under your own colors. Instead you appear in Kim's clothes, wearing her pearls, her perfume, perpetuating this disguise. I can only suspect you have some ulterior motive for impersonating your sister. Unless you convince me here and now that you haven't, you and I are going to pay a call on the police."

Kelly's mouth opened, but no sound came out. Unnerved, she sat staring into his intent blue eyes. At last she said sharply, "I've already visited the police station, not once, but twice, to ask Captain Creel to help me find Kim."

Eric's eyes widened in astonishment.

Indignation and outrage burned inside her. "As a matter of fact, I've wondered just exactly what *your* interest in my sister is. For all I know she could have gone skiing with you, met with an accident, fallen to her — her death, and you, unwilling to accept the blame, or unable to find her, are sitting back waiting for someone else to find her."

Eric drew back from the table and sat stiffly erect, staring at her in appalled silence. Clearly, that he himself could be suspect had never occurred to him. A stricken expression came into his eyes. "I cannot allow myself to think Kim has met with an accident!"

Kelly's heart went out to him. She had absolutely no reason to believe Eric wished Kim harm, and his concern for her appeared genuine. In fact, the glow that lighted his face when he spoke of her was the look of a man in love. Feeling suddenly sorry for him, she went on gently. "I thought if I impersonated Kim, whoever caused her to leave would react, and maybe I'd learn why she's taken off."

"And *has* anyone reacted?" asked Eric soberly.

Kelly's lips curved in a rueful smile. "*Everyone* has reacted. You, your friend Lauren Duval, others of the aprèsski crowd, but most of all, one of the salesmen at Alpenstock where Kim works — worked." A worried light came into her eyes. "He thinks she stole something from the company."

"That's ridiculous!" Eric exclaimed.

"Of course! But I've no way of proving she hasn't, unless — until I find her."

"Are the police looking for her?"

Kelly gave a doubtful shake of her golden-blonde head. "I hope so. I filed a missing person's report, but the police don't inspire me with confidence." Kelly smiled into Eric's eyes. "Sergeant Gilmer is convinced she has a 'boyfriend' and has gone off with him on a skiing trip."

Eric's tanned features darkened in an angry flush. He brought his fists down on the table in a decisive thump. "I'm her 'boyfriend,' as they put it. I'll go down there first thing in the morning and set them straight on that theory. How else have you tried to find her?"

Just then a waitress brought their order, and while they ate Kelly told Eric all that had happened since she'd arrived at Blue Angel, ending with the search she and Brad had made of the ski tour trails.

"How about you?" Kelly asked. "Have you looked for her?"

Eric shot her a sheepish grin. "We had a — a disagreement over the ski tour. You see, I didn't want her to go. When the tour ended and she didn't appear for her ski lessons, I supposed that she was showing me — how do you say it? — the cold shoulder. It wasn't until you came to the lodge masquerading as Kim that I really began to worry. I said nothing to you that night because I was waiting to see the game you were playing." He shrugged, extending his hands in a futile gesture. "Nothing seemed to be happening.

"I tried to call you last evening and all day today to have a serious talk with you, because I myself intended to tell the police that Kim is missing — but you were gone. Tomorrow I will go and tell them she's not off with me on a skiing holiday." His open, honest face contorted in a frown. "She is rather a loner, you know. She spends all her free time tracking down her ancestors and, lately, dating me and taking ski lessons, but I'll ask the other students if they know where she might have gone."

While they talked the tables had filled with diners. The room hummed with loud chatter and laughter. At the far end, perched on a tall stool at the edge of a small dance floor, a guitar player strummed a country-western tune. Kelly leaned across the table toward Eric, trying to make herself heard above the din.

"Do you know that Kim actually went on the ski tour?"

"I know she signed up for it — I assumed she'd gone."

"My friend spoke to the director on the phone. She couldn't remember Kim — there were so many . . ."

Eric nodded. "That's understandable. Tomorrow I'll see the director myself, refresh her memory about the cross-country tour so we can eliminate the possibility of Kim's having met with a real or so-called accident on the trail." His mouth curved in an infectious boyish smile. "You had best come with me, so she can see who we're looking for."

"I'll be happy to," agreed Kelly eagerly. The feeling she'd had looking at his picture on Kim's bookcase returned. Here was a man a mother would trust with her daughter. She felt she could trust him completely. "Did Kim talk with you about her research on the Conovers? I mean, did she ever mention anything unfavorable about any of them, or any other Blue Angel families?"

Eric shook his head. "Not that I can recall. If anything comes to mind, I'll let you know."

Warmly she said, "I can't tell you how much better I feel, knowing you're as concerned about Kim as I am, that someone else is on my team."

His grin widened. Reaching across the table, he clasped her slender hand in his, raised it to his lips, and, with elegant, old-world grace, kissed the back of her hand. He leaned forward, his head close to hers, smiling into her eyes. "Then we're friends and allies?"

Kelly returned his smile. "Friends and allies."

"Then let us enjoy the evening. After inviting you here under false pretenses, and judging your motives unjustly, I wish to make amends. I think Kim would wish it, too." He nodded toward the dance floor. "Would you care to dance?"

Feeling greatly cheered by the dinner discussion, Kelly gave herself over to enjoying a brief respite, following Eric in a Texas two-step to the lilting strains of the guitar. Eric was a marvelous dancer. She was enjoying herself thoroughly until she heard a loud, exuberant laugh somewhere over her left shoulder. Her head spun around. Not six feet away, as though he'd been born dancing, was Brad York, whirling around the floor, holding Lauren Duval close in his arms.

The girl was wearing a spaghetti-strapped top over skintight neon-pink satin slacks, guaranteed to attract attention. Lauren smiled flirtatiously up into Brad's rapt face. Kelly felt something green and unlovely writhing inside her. Brad must have followed her here, and that female piranha must have picked him up in the lounge.

Had Brad seen her dining with Eric? Seen him kiss her hand with eloquent Continental charm, their heads close together? At that moment, as if sensing her thoughts,

Brad glanced up, meeting her gaze. Gritting her teeth, Kelly shot him a look that could have felled a sentinel pine with one stroke.

Amusement sparkled in his dark eyes. He smiled expansively and gave a slight nod of his head, acknowledging her presence. Then, as though helplessly enchanted, he turned back to Lauren Duval. Eric's wry chuckle distracted Kelly's attention.

"Leave it to Lauren to latch on to the handsomest man in the lodge."

Kelly's brows rose in mild astonishment. "From the way she latched on to you last week with the après-ski crowd, I thought you and Lauren were probably engaged."

Eric laughed. "If we are, I'm unaware of it. Before Kim came along, I dated Lauren now and again. She's beautiful, amusing, diverting, but I never had serious intentions toward her. I'm afraid she doesn't understand that an instructor tries to be gracious and charming to all the guests, all his students, at Blue Angel Lodge."

"I hope Kim understands it."

A rapturous expression came over his face. "Kim is different. Quiet, composed, self-contained. Like no woman I've ever met before. Like an oasis in the desert. I detest loud, aggressive women — and I meet many of them. When I marry, it'll be to a warm, sharing woman who will be a partner in life as well as in love." A fond, dreamy expression lighted his eyes. "Kim is a wood nymph, a nature lover, like myself. A rare find! Do you wonder that I'm so upset over her disappearance?"

The music ended and they returned to their table. They had scarcely sat down when a jovial voice at Kelly's elbow said, "There seems to be a shortage of tables. Mind if we join you?"

Kelly glanced up to see Brad grinning broadly at Eric, Lauren clinging to his arm. Welded to his side like a Siamese twin, thought Kelly savagely. Lauren's cold blue eyes gleamed with the light of conquest.

"Please do," said Eric warmly. "Our pleasure."

Speak for yourself, Eric, thought Kelly, forcing a stiff, welcoming smile. The pleasure is all yours. Coolly she introduced Brad as her houseguest. Graciously Eric rose, extended a hand to Brad, then pulled out a chair for Lauren.

Once they were seated, Lauren took over, talking of the merits of the various ski areas at Blue Angel, and boasting of her own expertise on the advanced runs.

When she paused to take a breath, Kelly started to speak, but Lauren leaped into the gap, effectively excluding her from the conversation. Fuming inside, Kelly said nothing, a smile fixed on her lips. She caught Eric watching her, and from the perceptive glint in his eyes she knew he realized that she and Brad had something going. *Had* had something going, she amended quickly.

As she gazed at Lauren, the thought flashed through her mind that here was a vicious, predatory woman, determined to capture a man. A woman who was not above giving Kim a swift shove down a dangerous slope to scare her off skiing for good, or to cause her more serious harm. That would certainly explain Lauren's astonishment at seeing Kelly at the Italian Grotto the night she arrived. But then, Lauren hadn't gone on the ski tour — had she? Kelly tucked the disturbing thought away in a corner of her mind. It would bear looking into.

When at last they had said all that could be said about Blue Angel Mountain, Lauren turned a mocking gaze on Kelly.

"My, aren't you quiet this evening? Have you nothing to say? But you're only a novice skier, aren't you?" With a small scornful laugh, she went on in condescending tones, "I hope you've learned something that will be helpful — if you ever advance to an intermediate slope."

Brad said, "Oh, Kelly skis quite well." A glimmer of amusement shone from his dark eyes. "In fact, I doubt there's a slope in the world she can't negotiate. Kelly's an expert skier."

Lauren stared at Kelly with an expression of astounded annoyance. *"Kelly!"*

Looking at Lauren, Eric replied smoothly, "Sorry, I forgot you two hadn't met." Smiling, he placed a hand over Kelly's on the table. "This is Kelly Conover, Kim's twin sister."

"You mean there are *two* of you!" said Lauren in tones of mingled dismay and irritation.

"Double trouble," said Kelly sweetly.

Brad shook his head, his mouth quirking at the corners. "You can say that again!"

Kelly shot him another tree-felling glare.

Swiftly Eric put in, "And double the pleasure as well, to know two such lovely ladies." He gazed admiringly at Kelly, his hand tightening on hers.

Brad's eyes narrowed, his lips thinned. Kelly smiled inwardly, gratified to see that Eric's gesture wasn't lost on him. For once she was glad Brad never missed a trick. She looked up into Eric's face, smiling admiringly.

"Eric, you are so gallant. You've no idea how much we American girls appreciate your Continental charm."

The corners of Brad's mouth turned downward, a grimace he sometimes made when faced with a rich dessert topped with too much whipped cream. Lauren glared at Kelly with undisguised venom.

Eric, intercepting Lauren's glance, took Kelly's hand firmly in his. "I think the music is about to begin. Let's dance before the floor becomes too crowded."

With an inward sigh of relief at escaping Lauren's and Brad's unwelcome company, Kelly rose from the table and let Eric lead her past the tables to the dance floor. Unaccountably her heart ached. The evening was all out of kilter, her respite spoiled by Brad York's following her here. Why did it never occur to that egotistical creature that there were actually times when his electrifying presence wasn't wanted! In fact, when he danced with her she would tell him so, in no uncertain terms! He was like a noxious weed, she thought savagely — no sooner had she stamped him out in one place than he popped up in another!

To Kelly's chagrin, her chance to tell him anything in no uncertain terms never came. The evening dragged dismally on, with

Lauren monopolizing the men, and Brad never once asked her to dance. How could he? she asked herself crossly. Lauren dragged him onto the dance floor at every opportunity — and when they were seated at the table, she kept up a bright, bubbling chatter so he couldn't get a word in. Still, in her heart, Kelly knew the day would never come when Brad couldn't get a word in — if he truly wanted to.

It was well after midnight, when Kelly suggested it was time for the party to break up. After she and Eric bid Lauren and Brad a cheerful good-night, Brad lingered at the table with Lauren. Kelly could have hit him.

Eric insisted on driving her back to the chalet, promising he'd drive her car over tomorrow. After his call on Captain Creel, he would pick her up at ten and they would go together to see the tour director. If Eric noticed her silence all the way home, he gave no sign of it. She supposed he thought she was feeling depressed over Kim's being gone — and she was — but at the moment she was thinking vengeful thoughts about Brad York's spending the entire evening playing up to that siren in neon-pink skin. He would have to go, that's all there was to it. She could scarcely wait for him to come back to the chalet so she could tell him so!

Eric escorted her to the door, then bent down and kissed her on the lips — a kind, comforting, brotherly kiss. He patted her shoulder, saying, "Don't worry, I'll help you find Kim," and was gone. Although she appreciated his reassuring gesture, she couldn't help thinking that there was a world of difference between his kiss and Brad's. She suppressed a sigh. She had felt none of the thrill, the fluttering of her heart that she always felt when Brad kissed her — but then she hadn't expected to.

She unlocked the door and stepped inside, feeling weary and defeated and angry, all at the same time. She could hardly wait to dive into bed, fall asleep, and forget for a short while that Kim was gone and that Brad York had acted like a perfect wimp the entire evening! But she couldn't fall asleep until Brad came home and she could speed him on his way.

She stamped up the stairs to the loft, undressed, and fell into bed. Wide-eyed, she lay listening, waiting for Brad to come in. Time dragged past. Where was he now? What was he doing? No need to wonder with whom, she thought dismally. She rolled and tossed until at last sleep overtook her.

Chapter Thirteen

Kelly awoke in pitch darkness to the comforting feeling of Brad's furred shins warming the calves of her legs. Drowsily, forgetting her resolve to tell him to move on, she rolled over, reaching for him. Her arms embraced warm air, a plump pillow. The space beside her was achingly empty. Disappointment, followed by swift indignation, coursed through her. Brad was still out with that — that pink panther! She sat up in bed and threw back the blanket. A rough purr pulsed through the darkness, a soft, furry form swept past her arm.

She let out a hushed cry. "Cleo! You rascal!" As she picked up the cat the fact that Cleo was here, upstairs, struck her. Her hands froze around the warm, sleek body.

Someone had let the cats out of the kitchen. Who? If Kim had come home, she'd have awakened her.

She sat motionless, clutching the cat, listening. Was Smythe making good his threat to "deal with her later"? Had he broken in through the garage, sneaked inside the house, up the stairs into the kitchen? Was he even now tiptoeing past the dining room, through the living room, heading up the stairs? Maybe he had seen the Mustang outside the lodge, or seen Brad, and thought they were both still there. Even worse, maybe he'd seen her leave, alone. Or maybe he'd come back to search the house again. She strained her ears, listening. She could hear nothing except Cleo's loud purr, buzzing like a band saw through the darkness. Cleo slipped from her grasp. Heart pounding, she could almost feel Smythe's long, strong fingers closing around her neck, choking her. She couldn't simply sit here, waiting for him to find her.

She leaped from the bed, raced to the armoire, and, parting Kim's clothes, plunged inside. She sat hunched on the floor, her back braced against the side, her knees drawn up under her chin. Quickly she pulled the door closed, praying that if Smythe thought to search the armoire, Kim's clothes would hide her. Hardly daring to breathe, she sat listening for footsteps on the stairs, waiting for the door to fly open. A suffocating silence settled around her.

Minutes passed, seeming like hours. She grew hot. Her hands were damp, her forehead beaded with perspiration. The air, fragrant with Kim's perfume, was warm and stuffy. She had no idea how much time had passed before she summoned her courage and pushed the door open a crack. Nothing stirred, not even the cats. Warily she poked her head out, listening. Once again she heard a vigorous purring throbbing through the silent house. Her brow furrowed in a puzzled frown. No cat in creation had ever purred that loudly! Curiosity consumed her.

Cautiously she crept from the armoire and crawled to the railing bordering the loft. The soft vibrating sound grew louder, throbbing upward. Every nerve ending tingled with fear. She pressed a cheek against the railing and peered down through the wooden slats into the living room. She drew in her breath sharply. In a shaft of moonlight shining through a slit between the drawn draperies, she saw the long, lanky body of Brad York stretched out on the couch under Kim's afghan, snoring peacefully. The cats were curled in the curve of his arm, snoozing.

Kelly felt a quick surge of anger sweep through her. For the last half hour she'd been scared silly, running for cover like a frightened rabbit, sure her life was in danger. All the time it was only Brad — Brad who had let the cats out and lay there snoring like a sleeping lion!

Be fair, she told herself silently. It was really your own imagination that sent you into hiding, not Brad. Perversely she was more put out with him than ever. Not only had he outstayed her at the lodge, he hadn't come upstairs to kiss her good-night. If he had, none of this would have happened. Furious at him, she was more furious at herself for caring. Never mind that she'd made perfectly clear at the lodge that she was angry with him. Fuming, she glared down at him. He probably thought, and rightly so, that it was wise to keep a safe distance from his irate hostess. If she'd had any earlier doubts about sending him away, she had none now. In fact, she should roust him out this minute and send him packing. She pushed down the thought that she wouldn't, couldn't, admit to herself: what she truly feared was that he'd work his charm on her. Now she had the incentive she was looking for. "First thing in the morning, my friend, you're going to put on your boots and go!"

Kelly overslept. She woke with a start,

glancing at the clock on the bedside table. Almost ten, she thought distractedly. She'd meant to send Brad on his way long before Eric came to pick her up. She slid from the bed and ran to the banister. Her hands tightened around the railing in dismay. Stunned, she stood gazing down into the living room. Brad was gone. There were no gloves, no scarf, not even his baseball cap, not a sign of him in sight.

Her hands dropped to her sides. At last she'd convinced him they were through, that there was nothing worth saving between them. Inexplicably a deep sadness flooded through her. She felt bereft, desolate. A stab of jealousy prickled inside her as another thought struck home. He could have gone to see Lauren. In either case, she should feel elated. Instead she felt like bursting into tears. Sternly she told herself that tears never solved anything. She must get on with her life, and finding Kim was the most important thing in her life right now. She'd better dress, to be ready to go with Eric.

She had donned a warm brown sweater and slacks and was brushing her hair before the mirror when she heard the front door open. Was Eric in the habit of just walking into Kim's chalet? she wondered. In mild surprise she crossed to the railing. She saw no one, yet she was sure she'd heard the front door open and close. Maybe Eric was looking for her in the kitchen. She dropped her brush and ran downstairs.

At the foot of the stairs she rounded the corner of the couch and stopped short. At her feet crouched a tiny, lost-looking white kitten. Around its neck, on a blue ribbon, hung a small, white tag. She picked up the kitten, cuddling it against her cheek.

Printed on the tag were the words **MY NAME IS** and in the blank space that followed was written: *SNOW WHITE. Please don't throw me out in the cold.* Below it was scrawled: *For my Blue Angel, with all my love, Brad.*

Kelly nuzzled the top of the kitten's head, stroked her back, unaware of the front door opening slowly behind her.

"You sweet thing! You're a darling!"

Over her shoulder a cheery voice said, "Did I hear someone mention my name?"

Kelly's head spun around. Brad, grinning with pleasure at Kelly's obvious delight in the kitten, stepped inside and closed the door.

Gazing up at him, she thought she saw a terribly vulnerable expression in his eyes that immediately disappeared. With mock severity she asked, "Are you a sweet thing? A darling?"

"What else?" he asked affably.

For a long moment she eyed him in silent appraisal. With a sudden flash of insight, the word *entrapment* popped into her mind. He was trying to worm his way into her good graces with a kitten, of all things!

She stood up, holding out the kitten, trying to thrust it into his arms. Swiftly his arms dropped to his sides. "Brad, thanks, but no thanks. I really can't accept this — this animal. All I need right now is another cat."

Brad smiled his most disarming smile. "That's just what I thought." With great charm, clearly lying, he went on. "So when I found this stray, I thought: Kindhearted Kelly will take in this poor homeless creature." He smiled expansively. "I go with it, naturally. Love my cat, love me. That's my newest slogan, created just for you."

"Brad, I am not interested in your newest slogan, or your cat, or you! How many times do I have to tell you?" She thrust the kitten toward his chest, threatening to let it fall. Quickly he closed the distance between them, curving his arms around her, the fluff of white fur nestled between them.

"Countless times, my love, I never tire of hearing your sweet voice."

"Brad, you are absolutely impossible."

"I never denied it." His lips came down on hers, warm and loving. When she started to protest, he said, "That's enough talk. Time for action."

When she could draw a breath, she blurted, "Brad, you're smothering the kitten."

With one quick motion he scooped up the kitten and set it on the floor, then locked his arms tightly around her, hugging her close to his chest.

"May nothing come between us forevermore!"

"Brad," said Kelly breathlessly, "you're squeezing the life out of me!"

He grinned down at her. "I'm a senior lifesaver, among other fine attributes. All you need is a little mouth-to-mouth resuscitation." His mouth came down on hers. She compressed her lips in an unyielding line and tried to push him away, but her arms were pinned to her sides, imprisoned in Brad's ardent embrace.

She opened her mouth to protest, and his lips closed over hers in a long, lingering kiss. Her knees went limp, giving way. Brad's arms tightened around her, lifting her off her feet, molding her body to his. Seemingly of their own volition, her arms closed about his waist, clinging to his lean, muscular frame. Waves of desire pulsed through her. His lips parted hers, seeking, demanding. She felt as though she were floating on a vast sea, like a small ship cut adrift from the rest of the world. Carrying her with him, Brad eased onto the couch. She felt a heady sensation of sinking, swirling downward, caught in a whirlpool of passion from which there was no escape. A delicious languor stole over her. Helplessly, hopelessly, she was drowning in his love, and loving every minute. Brad caressed every curve and crevice with his warm, gentle hands, at first soothing then arousing, exciting, inflaming her with feverish longing.

Her languor dissolved. Desire exploded within her. With joyous abandon she gave herself over to the rapture of matching Brad's passion, his fervent caresses, so that she had no awareness of time passing, or how long it was before she became aware of a vigorous pounding on the front door.

Abruptly she sat up, straightening her sweater, smoothing her hair. Brad pressed her down against the cushions, his face buried in the soft curve between her neck and shoulder. "It's the Avon lady," he murmured. "Ignore her and she'll go away."

Kelly sat up, pushing Brad from her. "It's not the Avon lady, it's Eric."

Brad pushed her down again, his chin planted firmly on her forehead. "Ignore Eric and he'll go away."

Kelly slid from Brad's eager embrace and went to the door. In brisk tones she said, "Eric will *not* go away. We're going to meet the ski tour director, to see if she remembers seeing Kim on last week's cross-country."

She opened the door and invited Eric inside. Between Brad, flushed-faced, hot-eyed, looking distracted, and herself, a bit too bright-eyed and cordial, it must have been obvious to Eric that he'd interrupted something. While Eric and Brad sat in the living room regarding each other like two strange dogs, making stiff, polite small talk, Kelly donned her hat, jacket, scarf, and gloves. With a grudging smile, Brad saw them to the door and managed a grumpy "Good luck!"

Kelly sat behind the wheel of the Mustang, Eric at her side, cruising toward the base lodge.

Chuckling, Eric said, "I don't think your friend Brad approves of me."

Kelly laughed. "It isn't that he doesn't approve of you. He has the misguided impression I'm going to marry him, and he doesn't approve of my going out with you.

He's afraid you'll forget I'm Kelly and not Kim."

At the mention of Kim, an expression of anxiety suffused Eric's round, ruddy face. "I might — if I weren't so damned worried about Kim."

"Don't sound so discouraged — you'll drag me down with you. I'm having enough trouble trying to stay calm. I'm really counting on your friend the director, that the minute she sees me she'll have total recall."

The tour director, Susan Thompson, was waiting for them in the cafeteria at the base lodge. She was a tall, big-boned woman with a mop of curly brown hair and sparkling gray eyes, wearing Blue Angel ski togs. With supple grace she rose from a table, extending a hand in greeting to Eric. She turned her attention to Kelly. Her lips curved in a hearty smile, dimpling her rosy cheeks.

Watching her intently, Kelly saw a gleam of recognition light her gray eyes. She could feel her heart beating in her throat. Here, at last, was someone who had seen Kim, might know where she'd gone.

Susan's gaze swept over her. She shook her head. "I can't believe how closely you resemble your sister! I remembered her the minute I saw you."

Mingled joy and optimism flooded through Kelly as she perched on the edge of her chair, listening while Eric, seated next to Susan, explained about Kim.

Susan kept nodding her head, saying, "I see, I see." When he had finished, she asked, "What would Kim have been wearing?"

Inwardly, Kelly winced at Susan's unfortunate choice of words — *would have been.*

"Probably the outfit she wears to class," Eric said, "Blue Angel parka and ski pants."

Kelly interrupted. "We can't be sure about that, Eric. There are Blue Angel ski togs hanging in her closet. She may have been wearing something else — something new bought for cross-country skiing. If so, I've no idea what it is."

Susan looked down at the table, as if to avert Kelly's hopeful gaze, nodding her head. "I see. I see."

"Kim did sign up for the tour, didn't she?" Kelly asked.

Susan glanced up at Kelly, meeting her anxious eyes. "Oh, she signed up all right. I checked that when your friend called about her. But whether she went along with us I really can't say. You see, there were so many in the group, twenty-five or thirty, and most of them wore caps, and goggles, and bandanas to protect their faces . . ." A sympathetic expression shone in her gray eyes and she extended her hands, palms up, in a helpless, apologetic gesture. "I'm sorry I can't help you."

An empty, futile feeling surged through Kelly, a feeling of despair that threatened to overwhelm her. With a supreme effort of will, she managed a smile. "I'm sorry, too, but thanks for trying. I'll have to find another trail to follow. I'd better be on my way." She bid them a hasty goodbye and left.

Once in the car, she sat motionless, staring into space, feeling unutterably depressed. It was all very well to say she'd find another trail to follow, but what trail? She'd have a real fight on her hands, trying to see Alpenstock's books, and the police would be the last to help her. And besides, she wouldn't know what to look for. That left the genealogy.

She had started out trying to find Kim by following in her footsteps. Kim had noted in her journal that she'd traced their family through courthouse records. A discouraged sigh escaped her. What could she learn that Kim hadn't already ferreted out? In desperation, she turned on the ignition and spun away from the lodge, steering the Mustang toward town.

It was almost noon when she mounted the steps of the two-story sandstone courthouse and marched purposefully through double, white wooden doors into a dimly lighted hallway smelling of oiled wood and pine disinfectant. Steam radiators hissed and crackled, but at least the place was warm. She paused, looked around, then headed toward a doorway over which hung a wooden sign: **RECORDS.**

A short, thin, white-haired man with hollow cheeks and thick-lensed glasses presided over a chest-high counter of dark, polished wood. Behind him stood rows of tall shelves holding an impressive collection of bound records.

Smiling, Kelly said, "I'd like to see the census report, beginning with the year 1860."

The old man shook his head. "Haven't got any census. Hafta get that from the fed'ral gov'ment. They've got all them records stashed away someplace in an archives."

She tried to keep her voice calm and even, but her tone betrayed her disappointment and frustration. "I'm trying to track down my family, the Conovers, who settled here in the 1850s. My great-great-grandfather was given a land grant in 1862 . . ."

In surprisingly strong tones, as if happy to be of help, he said, "Oh, you want to look at one of the property tax books." He turned from the counter and ambled back among the shelves, running a gnarled finger across the spines of the thick cardboard-backed books until he found the one he wanted. He lugged it across to the counter and dropped it down in front of her.

"Starts with 1876 when Colorado joined the Union — but we only have this one. Rest are in Denver for safekeeping." He nodded toward a long oaken table and two slat-back chairs standing under a high narrow window. "You can take it over there and study on it awhile."

Kelly thanked him, picked up the book, carried it to the table, and sat down. Sunlight spilled through the window, matching her anticipation. She was about to discover something important; she could feel it in her bones.

Carefully she leafed through the brittle pages, scanning the old records inscribed in neat, spidery script, the ink faded to a pewter-gray. Turning the pages one at a time, she scrutinized them for the name Conover. With growing impatience, she proceeded through the C's in the musty old volume. As she turned the next page her fingers froze. She stared down in dismay, unwilling to believe the evidence of her own eyes. She spread the book wide on the table, flattening the pages. Deep in the binding, clean sharp edges, as if cut with a razor, were all that remained of the pages that belonged there. She leafed through to the back of the book, hoping whoever had cut them out had put them back. All in vain.

She jumped up from the table and crossed to the old man. In agitated tones she said, "The pages I want to see are missing from that book! Did someone take them out to make a copy?"

The man gazed at her in astonishment. "We don't let anybody take pages out of our books."

Her voice grew high and shrill. "But they're gone!"

The old man shrugged and looked away, as if wishing she would disappear and not make waves. "If they're gone, they're gone, and I don't know anything about it."

Kelly's shoulders slumped in defeat. Wordlessly she crossed to the table, picked up the book, set it back on the counter, and went out. Who could have cut out those pages? Kim? An anxious flush stained her cheeks. Even more puzzling than who, was why?

She drove back to the chalet feeling utterly stymied. She had come to another dead end. Brad would have thought of something else to do. She almost wished he were here. No matter, she would think of something herself.

Chapter Fourteen

As Kelly mounted the steps to the chalet, the door flew open. Waiting inside, a welcoming smile lighting his face, stood Brad. In spite of herself she felt both happy and relieved to see him standing there.

His thick dark brows rose several notches. "News?"

She shook her head, her lips compressed in a grim line.

Brad's smile faded. "No luck at all?"

"No luck, either with the tour director or with the tax records at the county courthouse." She swept off her hat and gloves, unwound her scarf from her neck, shrugged out of her jacket, and tossed them all on the couch. She felt a coldness around her heart that had nothing to do with the freezing temperature outside. Perversely she wished Brad would take her in his arms and hold her tight. Shivering, she wrapped her arms about her. In despondent tones she went on. "The tax books are there, but the pages I need are gone."

"Gone!" he exclaimed.

Close to tears, Kelly nodded. "Someone got there before I did."

"That's a damned shame." He draped an arm about her shoulders, leading her toward the kitchen. "Look, I have lunch waiting. Come have something to eat, and tell me about it."

Wordlessly she sat down at the table. Brad pulled two plates of thick juicy hamburgers and French fries from the oven and set them on the table. He took a bowl of coleslaw from the fridge, poured two mugs full of steaming hot coffee, and dropped onto a chair across from her.

She stared down at the food he'd placed before her. "I didn't know you could cook!"

He grinned, his right eye closing in an amiable wink. "I don't tell you everything. I'm a man of many hidden talents. One of the things I do best is order takeouts from the deli."

Kelly laughed, thinking Brad could bring a smile to the lips of a sphinx. She took a sip of coffee, then bit into her hamburger. She had thought she wasn't hungry. Suddenly she was ravenous.

Brad, munching his hamburger and French fries, waited till she had downed several more bites, then, eyeing her soberly, said, "Speak."

Kelly shook her head. "There's really nothing to tell. The entire morning was wasted." She recounted her meeting with Susan Thompson and the news that there was no way of knowing for sure if Kim had gone on the ski tour. "What do you make of that?"

Brad shook his head. "If she didn't go, maybe something more important came up. I don't think you can read anything more into it."

Wearily she continued, telling him how the pages had been cut from the bound record book; that the clerk was no help at all. She gave a discouraged shrug. "That's it!"

Scowling, Brad let out a low whistle. "Well, the bad news is that the pages are missing. The good news is that there has to be a reason." His brows drew together in thoughtful contemplation. "If Kim ripped them off, it tells us something."

Kelly drained her mug of coffee and set it down firmly on the table. "Tells us what? I'm not getting the message."

His eyes narrowed, as if in deep concentration. "Tells us that Kim wasn't lost on the cross-country tour, isn't wandering around in the wilderness, or lying buried deep in some crevasse . . ."

Kelly tried to swallow over the sudden lump in her throat. "Not necessarily. She could have done both."

Brad gave an emphatic shake of his head. "No, too much of a coincidence. Pages missing, Kim missing, no way."

"The fact is, Kim is still missing." With an effort Kelly pushed down an insidious feeling of defeat rising inside her. She looked up at him, mute appeal in her eyes. "I'm fresh out of ideas. How about you?"

Brad gazed across the table at her, concern mirrored in his dark eyes. "You need something to take your mind off this for a while. You need to relax. Sometimes, if you take a break, you can come up with a fresh approach."

Kelly smiled ruefully. Brad's favorite place to relax was in bed. "What did you have in mind?"

Brad laughed. "Not what you're thinking. Driving back from the deli, I passed an old Victorian cottage that's been turned into a museum. Let's go look it over."

Kelly shook her head. "Kim might come home, or call. If she does, I want to be here."

Brad reached across the table and took both her hands in his, curving his palms around them, as if to warm them. His tone was gentle, persuasive. "If Kim were in trouble, we'd have heard something long before now. If she calls this afternoon, she can certainly call back. If she comes back, she'll still be here, waiting for us to come home."

Home? thought Kelly. It sounded strange to hear Brad speak of the place where they both were as "home." In other circumstances she'd have reminded him sternly that this was *not* his home, but at the moment the word had a rather comforting ring to it. She returned her attention to what he was saying.

"We can't sit here all day brooding about her." His hands tightened on hers. A beguiling light shone from his eyes. "Come on, Kelly. It'll do you good to get your mind off Kim for an hour or two."

Kelly's disconsolate gaze locked with Brad's. The prospect of sitting out the gloomy afternoon waiting was depressing. Besides, if they stayed here she should make good her threat to send Brad packing. Right now she wasn't in the mood to hassle him — or in the mood to be alone. With a small sigh of surrender she withdrew her hands from his and rose from the table. "Let's go."

The museum was housed in a quaint yellow Italianate cottage whose peaked roofs and dormer windows were trimmed with white latticework. A sign hanging on the door read: **BLUE ANGEL MUSEUM. OPEN THURSDAY TO SUNDAY, 1:00–5:00.**

Brad grabbed her hand, swinging her arm with his as they strode up the walk. Cheerfully, he remarked, "Museum's open, it must be Thursday."

"Or Friday, or Saturday, or Sunday," said Kelly brightly, trying to match his mood. "Here in the mountains, all the days seem to run together."

At the door they were welcomed by a slender red-haired woman in her twenties wearing a smartly tailored navy blue blazer, burgundy silk blouse, and gray slacks. A silver squash-blossom necklace graced her generous bosom, and a silver charm bracelet jangled on one wrist. Enthusiastically she explained that the museum was run by the historical society in an effort to preserve the heritage of the gold rush days when the town was founded. Kelly noted with wry amusement that her eyes never left Brad's face.

"It's also a tribute," said their guide, "a memorial to the hardy farmers and fortune seekers who hung on despite terrible hardships — pioneers, really." With obvious reluctance she left them alone to browse through the exhibits.

Kelly and Brad lingered before lighted glass display cases mounted on the walls and perused the free-standing cases arrayed about the room.

Kelly became engrossed in a display of clothing: miners' garb, women's feedsack skirts, long white petticoats, and drawers. Another case held hats, gloves, fur tippets, boots, and shoes.

They moved into a room filled with furniture: a platform rocker, a wooden bedstead, cradle, spindle-back chairs, a long pine table, a corner cupboard. Transported into another era, Kelly felt her worry and anxiety fade.

They ambled into a kitchen that looked as it might have looked at the turn of the century: a black iron cookstove, tin cups and pans, wooden bowls, a pie safe, a scarred dough trough, a gleaming cooper wood box, two glass-chimneyed oil lamps on the mantle over the fireplace. The last room housed a display of farm implements and placer mining gear: a battered plow, rakes and hoes, an assortment of tools, a sluice box, a sifter, cracked leather harnesses, a steel-rimmed wagon wheel.

Brad gave a dubious shake of his head. "I'm impressed, but I'll take New York,

New York, any day!" He strolled back into the front room.

Kelly stared about her in silent wonder, contemplating all the memorabilia that attested to the hardships her Conover ancestors and others had endured. We're a sturdy bunch, she thought, and we don't give up easily. The thought reassured her. No matter what sort of trouble Kim was in, Kim would never give up. Nor would she. She heard Brad's footstep, felt his arm close around her waist.

"We've seen everything down here." The corners of his mouth quirked in amusement. "But our guide tells me there's another room upstairs we mustn't miss."

Kelly grinned. "I don't want to miss anything. Let's go."

The room upstairs was an attic converted to a gallery whose whitewashed walls were hung with photographs lighted by brilliant sunshine streaming through the dormer windows.

They ambled past pictures of grizzled prospectors panning for gold, pale-faced miners packed on a cage to descend to the depths of a shaft, an old mill straggling down a mountainside, a cluster of miners' shanties, and several stately Victorian mansions. Other pictures portrayed the town in bygone days: a pharmacy, hotel, blacksmith's shop, bank, jail, opera house, and, Brad remarked, chuckling, "enough saloons to inebriate an army on the move."

They turned their attention to the glass cases standing in the center of the room, where they viewed a display of handbills, opera programs, and newspaper clippings. While Kelly leaned over the case, reading the names of a traveling cast on a program of *Macbeth*, Brad strolled on to the next display.

"Kelly, take a look at this!" His voice held a hint of suppressed excitement that made her hurry to his side. He pointed to a large yellowed square of paper on which was drawn a diagram bordered by figures, with a written description below. "This is a page from a bound volume showing a section of land acquired by the Walker family in 1862, under the Homestead Act. Isn't that how your family got their land?"

Kelly nodded, excitement kindling inside her. "Kim has the original land grant stashed away somewhere. I'd love to find out where it is — go to see it. Maybe that's what Kim has done — where she is now!" Clasping Brad's arm, she started down the stairs. "Let's ask the guide to show us the book this was taken from."

Brimming with anticipation and hope,

Kelly found the guide and stated her request. Slowly, regretfully, the woman shook her head.

"I'd be more than willing to show it to you, but the bound volume is kept in the library."

"The library," echoed Kelly eagerly. "Where's the library?"

"On Main Street, on the second floor of the firehouse." She smiled wryly. "It seemed the safest place — after all, these old books of plats are irreplaceable, and —"

Brad interrupted. "Well, thanks for the information. We'll head on over there."

The woman shook her head. "Won't be any use. It's closed today. The librarian is only there on Mondays and Wednesdays from two till five."

Kelly, clenching her fists in desperation thought, *Oh my God, this town is driving me out of my mind! Here another weekend is rolling by and now, when this could be it, I have to sit on my hands for three days!* Kelly took a deep breath in an effort to keep her voice calm and controlled. "Do you think she'd open up for us? It's terribly important."

"She might, if she were here, but the rest of the week she works in the Denver Library."

"Surely someone has a key, someone could let us in."

Again the woman gave a firm shake of her head. "We make no exceptions. Once you start, everyone has a special reason for visiting the library." She grinned, as if making a joke. "Of course, the fire chief has a key, but he'll open up only if the place catches fire, and that's hardly likely."

Brad's hand closed firmly about her arm. In dry tones he said, "I think we can make it through the weekend." He led her out to the car.

The weekend passed faster than Kelly would have believed possible. Brad did everything he could think of to divert her, to keep her mind occupied. They skied from early morning, on runs tinted rose by the rising sun, till dusk, on purple-shadowed slopes. On Friday night they dined at the Italian Grotto, lingering over their wine, reminiscing over old times, chatting of this and that. Kelly smiled inwardly, marveling that they never ran out of things to talk about.

On Saturday night Kelly cooked up a pot of spaghetti and tossed together a green salad while Brad slathered garlic butter on a loaf of Italian bread and put it in the oven to heat. They carried their plates into the living room and, sitting cross-legged before a blazing fire, devoured their meal. Brad filled wineglasses with rich, dark red Chianti again and again.

A mellow feeling stole over Kelly. "You're spoiling me, Brad."

He set her empty plate on the lamp table along with his own and, curving an arm about her shoulders, gave her a bearlike hug. Smiling down at her, a look of adoration in his eyes, he said, "There's nothing I'd rather do."

Almost regretfully she shook her head. "That was your first mistake."

He set his wineglass down on the table and placed his fingers under her chin, tilting her face up to his. Earnestly he said, "You're the girl I want! Nothing but the best, can you blame me?"

"Then why can't we go on the way we were: friends, enjoying each other's company, doing fun things together. Why rock the boat?"

Smiling, he gave a relentless shake of his head. "I want a lifetime contract. All or nothing."

She turned her head away, staring into the fire. "Brad, you're rich, successful, attractive, there's a world of women out there who'd give their eyeteeth to marry you . . ."

A short, ironic laugh escaped him. "Oh, absolutely. I'm rich, successful, attractive, and all my life I've knocked myself out proving myself — to whom? Who cares?"

"*You* care," said Kelly vehemently. "Nobody understands that better than I do. You have to prove to yourself that you've got what it takes to hack it in this world."

Brad gave a vigorous shake of his head. "I *know* who I am. I don't have to prove anything to myself — and no one else gives a damn. No one cares whether I come home at night, or worries that I've been in an accident, or if I'm lost, stolen, or strayed. I want someone to come home to, Kelly. That someone is you. You're the most caring person I've ever known."

A lump rose in her throat. She hadn't been mistaken about the vulnerable look she thought she'd seen in his eyes the morning he gave her the kitten. She put her arms around his neck and gazed up into his face. "I care about you, Brad. I'll always care about you — even if a lifetime contract isn't for me."

He kissed the dimple in her chin. His arms went around her, and his lips claimed hers in a defiant, demanding kiss, as if to belie her words. Gently she drew back from him and, relaxing against the curve of his arm, gazed moodily into the fire. It was pleasant and cozy, she thought, sitting here with Brad in this peaceful hideaway, far from the hectic hustle and bustle of New York — if only it could last forever. But she mustn't let herself think such thoughts. She was only enjoying a change of pace. But if that was so, why did the thought of returning to New York cause this strange hollow feeling inside?

As if sensing her disquiet, Brad took her hand in his. Smiling into her eyes, he lifted it to his lips and kissed her palm. She rested her head on his shoulder, felt the soft pressure of his chin on her hair and his warm, loving hands stroking the length of her back, sliding down over her hips. The hollow feeling inside her vanished, replaced by a sense of utter completeness. She lifted her face to his.

"Why is it, when I'm with you I always feel as if I'm home?"

Grinning down at her, he said softly, "Home is where the heart is — and home for me is wherever you are."

Before she could reply, his lips claimed hers in a long, lingering kiss. With a supreme effort of will she drew away from him. Through a daze of passion she murmured, "Brad York, you are deliberately seducing me! We've already had our night to remember!"

A dreamy expression came over his face. "And what a night it was, my love!" His lips curved in a smile that was both sad and beguiling. "Do you realize that tonight may be the last time we'll ever make love?"

Kelly felt a sinking sensation inside. A depressing thought, but one that had to be faced and dealt with. There *had* to be a last time, sometime. The sooner the better, and the easier it would be to see Brad walk out of her life. She gazed directly into his eyes, reading in their dark depths mingled pain and hope. Her heart thudded painfully as she spoke the words: "For the last time ever . . ."

He stretched out before the fire and drew her down beside him. He kissed her slowly, tenderly, as if savoring every moment, just as she herself was storing each caress in her memory to recall should she miss him, day or night. His gentle, loving hands explored every soft curve of her body, arousing in her a longing that only he could assuage. Slowly, deliberately, with gentle caresses, they eased off each other's clothes, their bodies blending, glistening with an ivory sheen. She wanted him with all her heart and soul.

Would she ever stop wanting him? Suddenly the aching knowledge that tonight would be the last they would ever be together lent a piquancy, an urgency to every embrace, enhancing their lovemaking in a way she had never known. Every nerve ending cried out for him to take her, yet he held back, as if to prolong the joy of anticipation to the peak of desire. When at last their bodies joined in an exquisite ecstasy, she felt swept away into another world, stirred by an emotion that touched the deepest recesses of her heart. As Brad murmured loving words, his lips soft against her own, she cried out his name, again and again. Never had she felt this way before, never would she feel this way again. At length, their passions sated, they slept in the faint red glow of the firelight.

On Sunday night after dinner at the Cafe Français, they came home and popped corn over a glowing fire in the fireplace, toasting their toes, their heads resting on Kim's afghan.

Shortly after ten, determined to avoid a repeat of last night's lovemaking that had left her shaken and longing for more, Kelly got to her feet, yawning widely. "It's been a long day. I'm going to turn in. You can make up your bed here on the couch, can't you?"

Brad cocked his head to one side, looking up at her with a provocative light in his eyes. "You bet!"

Quickly she turned away and climbed the stairs to the loft. She was almost asleep when Brad slid in beside her.

"Brad, I thought you were going to sleep on the couch."

"I am. I'm certainly not planning to *sleep* here in this marvelous king-size bed!"

Knowing better than to ask what he intended, Kelly sat up and glared at him in the cold, frosty blue moonlight sifting in through the window. In teasing tones she said, "Don't tell me you're afraid of the dark!"

"That's it! Why didn't I think of that? I'm afraid of the dark."

"Then go downstairs, close the drapes, and turn on the table lamp."

"In a minute, sweetie." He rolled over and took her in his arms. "Do you realize you forgot to kiss me good-night?"

Kelly let out an exasperated sigh. "Listen, Brad, when we made love last night, it was for the last time. You said so yourself."

"You said that, I didn't. If I did, I lied. Besides, last night was only a practice session. Tonight it's the real thing."

She let out a long, nostalgic sigh. *The real*

thing! What would her life be like if these last days with Brad were all a foretaste of the real thing? Not too bad, not bad at all. The next instant, intruding on her reverie, she envisioned all her ambitions, her hopes, her plans for Conover Executive Suites dissolving in air.

"Brad, darling," she murmured gently, "I hate to disillusion you, but our relationship is not the real thing at all — it's just pretend, only make-believe."

Propped on one elbow, he grinned down at her, tracing the outline of her lips with one finger. "And that's a paper moon shining through the window. Right?"

"Right."

Her brows drew together in a faint frown. She had a vague, unnerving feeling she'd come out on the short end of the discussion, but Brad's lips were warm on hers, his hands curving around her breasts, his thumbs moving over their taut peaks, his knee sliding seductively between her thighs. She wasn't thinking very clearly. In fact, she wasn't thinking at all. All she knew was that she hungered for him as she never had before. With mounting passion she ran her hands up and down the lean, muscular length of his body, pressing him to her as if she wished they could stay this close forever.

Still, the certain knowledge that they must part made these last days and nights together all the more poignant. No matter how much she rejoiced in Brad's lust for life; admired his calm, cool way of hanging in there no matter what; delighted in his laughing, loving, devil-may-care manner, she wished he'd move out of her life and stop turning her world upside down. "Brad," she said flatly, "tomorrow morning you have to go. No more hanging around."

"Right on," he murmured, his lips close to her ear.

With the matter settled once and for all, all thought left her. The next moment she became lost in the king-size bed, lost in Brad's loving arms.

Kelly awoke the next morning to the fragrant aroma of coffee brewing and bacon frying. She slipped on a white fuzzy robe and ran downstairs to the kitchen. Brad, fully dressed, a pink apron tied about his narrow waist, was standing at the stove flipping flapjacks.

Without looking at her he said morosely, "The last meal for the condemned prisoner of love."

Grinning, refusing to be taken in by his forlorn mien, she sat down at the table.

"How nice of you to share it with me."

Wordlessly he slid the plate of food onto the table and sat down across from her. A heavy stillness closed around them. It seemed to Kelly that there was nothing more to be said. They had said it all. They finished their meal in silence. Then, to Kelly's astonishment, without a murmur or protest, Brad excused himself, strode into the living room, and, without a word, packed up his gear and left.

A feeling of abandonment flowed through her. She felt suddenly bereft, as though someone had died. Somehow, when Brad was here, his presence filled the whole house. "It's just that the chalet seems so empty," she told herself. "Of course I miss him!" Sternly, she added, "Like an aching tooth that's been yanked out! Don't just sit here, *do* something!"

Spurred into action, she washed and dried the breakfast dishes. With a vengeance she pushed the vacuum cleaner around the small chalet, dusted the furniture, and threw a load of laundry in the washer, all the while keeping an eye on the clock, wishing the hands toward two, when the library opened. The morning dragged past with no word from Kim, or even Captain Creel. Her mind kept straying to Brad.

Firmly she told herself that the one and only unfortunate thing about his leaving was that he wouldn't be here to answer the phone, but her words lacked conviction. At quarter till two she went down to the garage, climbed into Kim's jeep, and drove toward town.

Chapter Fifteen

Kelly mounted the steps to the library and crossed to a desk labeled **MISS DUNWOODIE, LIBRARIAN**. Behind it sat a short, squat woman in a reddish-brown pants suit, with reddish-brown hair braided in a crown atop her head. Her bright brown eyes sparkled with interest as she gazed up at Kelly, the only patron in the light, spacious, book-lined room.

Eagerly Kelly asked to see the book of plats showing the land owned by early homesteaders.

"No problem," said Miss Dunwoodie, jumping up from her chair. Briskly she led Kelly across the room to a shelf labeled **COLORADO HISTORY**, pulled down several thick, black-backed, metal-bound volumes, and stacked them on a table.

Kelly sat down and began leafing through them, scanning the plats — maps, actually — of sections of land that had been deeded to early homesteaders, searching for the property once owned by her great-great-grandfather, Luther Conover. Head bent over the pages, she studied fascinating handwritten descriptions of "meets and bounds," delineating shapes and sizes of properties bounded by streams and creeks, fenceposts and foothills, crisscrossed by wagon roads. Within minutes, she became aware of her mistake. Swiftly she rose and faced Miss Dunwoodie across her desk.

Agitatedly she said, "These plats show no names of their owners. The one I saw in the museum gave the name of the owner and the date the property was purchased."

Miss Dunwoodie looked crestfallen. "Plats don't show the owner's name. The museum historian must have mislabeled the exhibit. You want the abstract of the property you're interested in. The abstract tells you the history of the ownership of the property, and —"

"Where will I find the abstract?" asked Kelly, barely able to control her impatience.

"The abstracts are on file in the courthouse. All you need to know is the present owner of the land. Then you can trace it back to the original owner. The abstract gives the volume and page number of the plat record, so you can come back here and look up . . ."

Kelly stopped listening. All she knew was

that her great-great-grandfather Luther Conover had owned one section of land, six hundred forty acres. She assumed that on his death it had passed down to his son Walter, then to his grandson Robert, and finally to John Conover, her father. Kelly knew her parents had never owned a section of land, so who *had* inherited the property? Her father's sister had died young, and his brother had been killed in the Korean War. A memory buried deep in her mind surfaced. Her grandfather had sometimes spoken of a ranch, owning horses; Pastor Meyer had told her that her grandparents had left Colorado in 1935. Her grandfather must have simply sold out! Her shoulders slumped in disappointment. There was no way she could know who now owned the land. No point in going to the courthouse and delving through abstracts.

Had Kim discovered the same thing she had? Was there more to be learned that would explain Kim's disappearance? Kelly shook her head in despair. She had traced the Conovers from their roots to the tip of the family tree, and she knew no more about Kim's whereabouts than when she'd begun her search. Disheartened at having reached another dead end, she thanked Miss Dunwoodie and left.

As she drove through town a sense of gloom settled over her. What could she do now but wait?

On the edge of town, as she swung right onto the graveled road leading to Alpine Village, a billboard caught her eye. Instead of the faded, peeling ad touting a local motel that she was accustomed to seeing, a new ad blazed across the board. Staring incredulously, she almost drove up on the curb, then slowed to a stop. She couldn't believe the evidence of her own eyes. A gigantic lace-trimmed scarlet heart bordered with forget-me-nots filled the billboard. Splashed across it in huge sky-blue letters were the words: **K. CONOVER IS SOMEBODY'S DARLING!**

Kelly burst out laughing. One thing she could say for him, Brad was never at a loss for words, even if he couldn't say them in person! Into her mind flashed a vision of Brad's laughing face, a loving look in his eyes, saying, "It pays to advertise."

Unaware that she was speaking aloud, she said softly, "Fine words will do you no good this time, my friend, because my sales resistance is tougher than any ad campaign you'll ever dream up!"

She gunned the jeep and pulled back onto the road. All the way home, conflicting feelings tormented her. She was by turns flattered, then furious; delighted, then distraught. With a small twinge of nostalgia, she wondered why the thought that Brad had gone out of her life was suddenly painful. Much as she hated to admit it, she missed him. Now, when there was nowhere else to search for Kim, what would Brad do? That, she knew! Brad would hang in there till he got what he wanted.

By the time Kelly pulled into the driveway back of the chalet, she knew what she'd do. She set her lips in a resolute line. She would call Captain Creel to see what, if anything, he'd done. If he had no news, she'd demand he send out a special detail to look for Kim. If he refused, she'd raise such a fuss he'd soon find out it was easier to go along with her than to put up with her hassling him day and night.

As she turned down the dirt road back of the chalet, chill winds buffeted the canvas top of the jeep. Shivering, she pulled up before the garage, wishing there were an automatic opener on the overhead door. She alighted from the jeep, ran to the door, gripped the chrome handle, and gave it a twist. At the same time a black-gloved hand shot over her right shoulder, closed over her wrist. A dark blue parka-clad arm curved around her left side, pinning her arm to her ribs, forcing the air from her lungs.

"Brad! You nut! You're squeezing me to death!"

"That would be a lucky break for you, sister," snarled a voice in her ear.

Her head spun around and she looked into the hard glittering eyes of Bill Smythe. "You!" she shrieked. "Let go of me!" She kicked out, landing a sharp blow on his shins with her booted heel.

He swore softly. "I've been waiting a long time to take you in. And now Teague's tired of waiting — sent me after you." His arms tightened around her as he dragged her backward across the ice-packed driveway, past the other chalets, to his black van parked around the corner at the end of the row.

She opened her mouth to scream. Smythe, anticipating her move, quickly clapped a hand across her lips. Wrenching open the door, he shoved her onto the seat and across to the passenger's side. He jumped in the driver's seat, started the motor, and slammed his foot down on the gas pedal. The van shot forward, throwing her back against the seat as it charged down the dirt road.

Frantically Kelly fumbled for the door

handle on her side. It wasn't there, where it should have been. He'd taken it off! The van careened onto the country road, spewing gravel.

"You're not as clever as you think," Kelly said. "My friend in the chalet is watching for me to come back. He probably saw you down there hustling me into your van and is out the front door, following you in my car."

Smythe sneered, "You're not as clever as *you* think. I checked the front of the house. Your boyfriend left hours ago . . . in your car."

"You're making a really stupid move, and it won't do you any good. You won't learn a thing from me."

She saw a nasty smile curve his lips. "Maybe I won't. But Clarke Teague will. He knows ways of dealing with people like you."

"Where are you taking me?"

"To where you won't cause any trouble. Now shut up."

She clamped her lips together, trying desperately to think how to get away. If only she could wind down the window, maybe she could open the front door from the outside. She kept her eyes on the road ahead, watching intently for a good place to jump from the van. Slowly she began to wind down the window, shielding her hand with her body. She gave a start. Far ahead, trudging along the side of the road, was a lone hiker, a pack on his back, bent into the wind. In faint, plaintive tones Kelly said, "It's hot and smelly in here. I feel sick." She continued to wind down the window.

Smythe's right arm flashed across her and came down in a hard chop on her forearm that stung to the bone. "Lay off the window, sister. If you're gonna be sick, grab that bucket on the floor behind you. Don't turn around, just reach for it."

Swiftly she stretched an arm down the narrow space between them, groping behind the seats. Her mind whirled, toying with a calculated risk. They were skirting a long snowy meadow. If she slammed the bucket down over Smythe's head, maybe he'd lose control of the van and she could get away. Even if the van careened into the meadow and turned over, her chances of landing unharmed were good. Forewarned, she would brace her hands against the dash. With a little luck, Smythe would be pinned behind the wheel and she could take off before he knew what happened.

Her groping fingers found the wire handle, swooped the bucket upward over the back of the seat — and her plan disintegrated. The bilious green plastic bucket was no larger than a three-pound coffee can.

The hiker was dead ahead. She dropped the bucket on the floor and spun to face the window, shouting, waving her hands. Again Smythe's arm shot out. His clenched fist landed a bruising knuckle blow on her upper arm. She cried out in pain.

"Any more smart-ass moves like that and I'm gonna tie you up." His menacing gaze dropped to several lengths of clothesline rope lying on the floor between them.

"My, aren't we brave!" snapped Kelly.

"Shut up!" Smythe yelled, glaring at her.

Kelly fell silent. It wasn't Smythe's words or his menacing tone that silenced her. It was the glint of pure evil burning in the depths of his small glittering eyes.

As the van began to climb through the foothills, past groves of aspen and dark spruce, Kelly's heart quailed. She had no reason to doubt Smythe's statement that Brad had gone off in her car. He had probably toted his gear out to his plane behind the chalets to convince her he was leaving town, then taken the Mustang to cruise around Blue Angel to look for another place to stay. She knew he'd be back to return her car. But when? When he did come back, would he let himself into the chalet, find her gone, and take off? Or would he plunk himself down on the couch to wait for her? How long would he be content to sit around, waiting? No one else would miss her, would even know she was gone. Her eyelids stung with tears of anger and vexation. Brad was her only hope of rescue, and she'd sent him away. If he never came back, she had only herself to blame.

Small, puffy cumulus clouds gathered overhead in great clusters, darkening the sky, as they ascended the steep, winding road up the south face of one of the Blue Angel Mountain peaks. She knew now where Smythe was taking her. At the thought she grew rigid with fear.

When Smythe swung off the road, down the rough dirt lane toward the mine, she envisioned the derelict shed, the seemingly bottomless shaft. No one would ever find her there. A flicker of hope burned feebly inside her. Maybe, just maybe, there would be enough water in the bottom of the shaft to break her fall. The water would be dark and icy cold, but maybe she could tread water, or float on her back till someone came to save her. But who would come? The numbing fear enveloped her, blocking out all thought.

Smythe parked the van in the driveway beside the faded red Victorian mansion and cut the engine. He slid out, ran around to the passenger's side, opened the door, and yanked Kelly out. She made no protest when he gripped her arm and dragged her stumbling across the snowy ground, up the steps, and inside the house. Furious, she thought there was no use fighting him now, when she had no hope of eluding him.

He pushed her ahead of him down a long dark hall. Through a doorway on her left she glimpsed a moth-eaten dark blue velvet Victorian sofa, two chairs, and a pie-crust–edged table littered with glasses, beer cans, dirty dishes and red-and-white-striped cartons from a take-out chicken stand. On her right was a room that must once have been a dining room, but now apparently served as an office. A massive round oak pedestal table held a black telephone, a typewriter, an adding machine, a scattering of papers, ashtrays filled with cigar butts, and more beer cans. A china cabinet was crammed full of manila folders, brochures, and maps.

Smythe led her into the dining room and pushed her down in a slat-back chair. He pulled up a chair alongside her, sat down, then picked up the telephone receiver. Grinning maliciously, he draped the long thin black cord in a noose around her neck, then dialed a number. A pleased, vindictive expression came over his lean, wolfish face.

Kelly heard a high, garbled voice on the other end of the line. "Alpenstock Land Development Corporation."

"Lemme speak to Teague." After a short pause he went on. "I've got her. Whaddya want me to do with her?" A longer pause. "Yeah. You leaving now? Okay, gotcha." He dropped the receiver back on the hook and turned to face her. Without unwinding the cord from her neck, he said, "Okay, lady. Where's your ever-lovin' sister?"

Kelly's voice bristled with irritation. "I told you before I don't know, and I still don't know."

"Look, lady, I didn't roll into town on a turnip truck. You've been here more than a week. Don't tell me your sister hasn't touched base with you."

Kelly shot him a scornful smile. "You're a slow learner, aren't you? I told you before, my sister doesn't know I'm here."

"Okay, so you just dropped by while you were out on your lunch hour one noon in New York. And while you were here, you found some things in that condo that don't belong to you or your sister. And you're gonna tell me where they are, or hand them over."

Kelly gave him an icy smile. "Oh, I'd be happy to, but one day while I was gone, a burglar rifled the chalet. He must have taken whatever it is you're looking for."

A dark red flush stained his thin, chiseled features. "Let's quit pretending you don't know what we're looking for. You hand over those files and the pages your sister lifted from our posting ledger if you ever want to see her again."

Fear spread through Kelly like acid. Did they have Kim then? Were they holding her prisoner somewhere, maybe in this house? She bit off her words, short and sharp. "I don't know where they are."

"Then you'd better tell us where your sister's hiding out or . . ."

Kelly felt as though the ground had dropped from under her. Conflicting emotions raced through her. This clod hadn't kidnapped Kim after all. Wasn't holding her prisoner somewhere upstairs. Wasn't planning to use Kelly as a hostage to force Kim to hand over those confounded papers they wanted. For one fleeting moment joy coursed through her, then evaporated. If these men didn't have Kim, where was she? In a fit of rage Kelly shrieked, "You stupid oaf. I don't know where she is!"

Fury contorted Smythe's features. "You damned lying bitch! You can't make me believe you don't know where your own sister, a *twin* sister, is! I ought to . . ." He glared at her malevolently. "And Teague won't believe it either." His lips curled in a sly smile. "He has ways of persuading you to talk. You'll talk to him, all right!"

It was then she understood the extent of his rage. He was furious because she wouldn't tell *him* what he wanted to know. Now he'd be forced to let Teague make her talk.

"And when Teague gets through with you, I'll have a go at you myself." Slowly his beady close-set eyes traveled the length of her body in a lewd, lustful stare that left no doubt as to what he had in mind.

Choking down terror, Kelly snapped, "You're really stupid, you know. Don't you think I'd tell you anything you want to know, give you your records or whatever they are, to save my sister, my *twin* sister?"

Smythe's lips turned down in a sour smile. "All I know is, you're not coming across. So help me, if you don't, Teague's gonna work you over. If he doesn't, I will!"

Kelly shook her head, feigning incredulity. "I can't believe anyone would be so dumb. If you kill me, you'll never get your records back, can't you see that?"

A broad sneer flashed across Smythe's face. "Can't you see that if we kill you and your sister, we won't *need* those records back!"

She didn't see, but pushing her advantage, she raged on. "So you'll add murder to your other crimes. That's *really* brilliant! You know who'll end up in prison? Not Clark Teague, upstanding citizen of Blue Angel. Oh no. You, Bill Smythe, will end up in jail!"

Smythe gave the black phone cord looped around her neck a vicious tug, pulling it tight. Her head jerked back violently, and she felt a strangling, choking sensation searing her throat. His free hand flashed out and landed a stinging slap across her cheek. "Quit mouthing off, you dumb broad, or you won't be *able* to answer Teague's questions!"

Her fingers clawed at the tight black cord, loosening it. She drew a raw, gasping breath. "You're angry now," she taunted, "because you know I'm telling the truth. You, not Teague, will serve time for murder. Teague will arrange it, guilty or not!" When she would have gone on to unnerve him further, she heard a car pull up outside, a door slam.

Moments later, a tall, beefy man wearing a black suit and a white shirt, his collar open and black tie askew, strode into the room. The man's stride, his stance, his jutting

256

chin, all radiated power, self-assurance, and a ruthless determination to take what he wanted.

Kelly was not surprised. Without knowing why, she had expected that Clark Teague would be the man who had stared at her so belligerently from the hotel steps the day she visited the cemetery. He stopped before her, his arms held stiffly at his sides, his hands balled into fists, the diamond flashing on his ring finger. He stared at her from half-lidded stony gray eyes, his thin, bloodless lips stretched across his teeth in a mirthless grimace.

Kelly steeled herself against him, staring back at him with a hot, hostile glare.

In whiplash tones he said, "You refuse to give us the papers your sister stole from my office?"

Kelly's unflinching gaze locked with his. "I don't have them."

"You refuse to tell us where your sister is?"

In tones as hard as his own, she retorted, "I don't *know* where she is."

Clark Teague stood staring at her for what seemed endless moments, as if weighing the truth of her words. At last he turned to Smythe. "Lock her in the room on the top floor. We'll keep her there till we find her sister. Later, when she's hungry and thirsty, we'll question her again. Her memory may improve."

Smythe's small weasel eyes burned with a feral gleam. He slipped the looped phone cord over Kelly's head and, gripping her arm, propelled her from the room. In the dim hallway he hustled her toward a narrow flight of dark wooden stairs that hugged the wall on her right.

"Up the steps and make it snappy," Smythe snarled.

Kelly shot him a scathing look. Squaring her shoulders, she mounted the stairs to the second floor. If she had to be locked up, she'd try for a front room where she could see who came and went. Recalling the low iron fence she had seen that surmounted the porch roof attached to the second story, she thought if only she could open the window . . . She stepped quickly down the shadowy hallway, past cabbage-rose wallpaper peeling from the walls. At once Smythe's fingers on her arm tightened in a cruel grip and spun her around.

"Hold it, sister." He nodded toward the stairway. "Up another flight. You're not climbing out any window and taking an afternoon stroll."

She set her jaw and climbed the steps,

with Smythe close as a shadow. She could smell his fetid, garlic-laden breath. At the top of the stairs he flung open a door that led into a circular room, empty except for a scarred four-poster bed. On the bed was a thin, lumpy mattress, its stuffing oozing from jagged tears in the filthy black-and-white-striped ticking.

The tower room! she thought, panicking. He's locking me in the tower! Wrenching free of his grip, she ran to a small dirt-encrusted window and peered out. She could see nothing below the broad expanse of the dull green-shingled porch roof. She wheeled to face him.

"Get out. Get out and leave me alone."

"Not so fast, sister." He crossed to her side and grabbed her wrist. "You go stretch out on that bed."

"No way!" Kelly shrieked.

His fist shot out, striking a blow on her chin that made her ears ring. He captured both of her wrists in one strong bony hand, dragged her to the bed, and flung her down on her back. With his free hand he dug in his parka pocket and pulled out the lengths of rope she'd seen in the van.

"Don't you dare tie me down!" Kelly shouted. "You can lock me up, but you can't tie me down!"

"The hell I can't, you mouthy bitch."

Kelly struck out at him with her fists, beating on his head, shoulders, and chest. Despite her struggles, faster than she would have believed possible, Smythe bound her hands and feet to each of the posts so she lay spread-eagle on the bed. She screamed, mindless hysterical shrieks that filled the room, echoing through the thin walls, throughout the old house. Furiously Smythe grabbed a wad of stuffing from the torn mattress and shoved it in her mouth.

In the sudden silence, Teague's irate voice came barreling up the staircase. "What the devil's going on up there?"

"Nothing!" shouted Smythe. "Nothing at all." He lowered his voice and bent over Kelly, his flushed, angry face close to hers. "But there will be, sister. You can count on it!"

He strode from the room, slamming the door. Kelly lay paralyzed with fear. She heard the click of a key turning in the lock, then Smythe's footsteps pounding down the stairs.

Chapter Sixteen

Panic engulfed her. Writhing, twisting, Kelly fought against the ropes that bound her wrists and ankles and burned into her skin, rubbing it red and raw. She gasped for air, choking, gagging on the cotton batting crammed in her mouth. Finally her panic subsided. She forced herself to slow her breathing, struggling to work the ropes loose. It was hopeless. Terror rose like a tide inside her. She grew faint with the crushing feeling of being captured. She felt disembodied, as if she were floating away, above the bed, over the housetop in vast endless space. Sure she was suffocating, her mind shut off.

Weak afternoon sunlight was creeping through the dirty window when Kelly gradually became aware of her surroundings. Angry shouts and a loud crash, as of a chair or table overturning, resounded up the stairs. Dully she thought, Teague and Smythe are having it out. Maybe they'll kill each other. There was a sudden silence, then the sound of footsteps pounding up the stairs. She stiffened, bracing herself for whatever was to come. A heavy weight hurled against the wooden door. Too heavy for Smythe — besides, Smythe had a key. It must be Teague. Again something, someone, crashed against the door. She squeezed her eyes closed, murmured a silent prayer. She heard a third violent blow, and the splinter of wood. As if ripped from its hinges, the door gave way, thudded to the floor. A voice shouted her name.

Her eyes flew open. Like a blast of wind in a winter storm, Brad burst into the room. Through glazed eyes, Kelly stared at him in astonished disbelief.

"Kelly, are you all right? Kelly . . ." His voice broke. In three quick strides he crossed to the bedside and bent over her, his features contorted in a frenzy of worry and fear. Gently he scooped the wad of stuffing from her mouth. She tried to speak, but her lips were stiff, her throat parched and raw. No sound came out. Brad placed his palms on her cheeks and lowered his face to hers, his cheek close to her lips, as if seeking the warm breath of life.

She lifted her head. Her lips brushed his flushed, anxious face. She made a small sound in her throat.

"Kelly! Oh God, you're all right! I was afraid . . ."

Kelly nodded, forcing her lips into a semblance of a smile. Her voice came out in a dry, whispery croak. "Brad, how did you know I was gone? How did you ever find me?"

As he spoke Brad's strong fingers grappled with the knotted ropes holding her captive. In tight, tense tones, he said, "I came back to the chalet to tell you I couldn't find a place to stay. You weren't there, but I saw the jeep parked out back. I went out to look for you and found the key in the ignition turned on. The jeep had run out of gas, so I figured *something* was wrong. I called your pal Captain Creel, who knew nothing. Then I drove to the Alpenstock office in town and demanded to see Teague. His receptionist told me he'd gone to the property site, so I drove straight out here. I took a shot in the dark and told Teague I'd come for you. He denied you were here, but Smythe looked guilty as sin. When I asked where you were and he wouldn't tell me, I hit him with a left on the jaw. Teague stood there with a superior smug look on his face, his lips drawn back over his teeth, like he was watching some boxing match on TV. Smythe folded like paper. I grabbed Teague by the collar and laid one on him, too, right between the eyes." Brad shook his head in mild surprise. "Teague's a tough customer. We staggered around and I finally winged him with a chair to bring him down." Brad strapped off the last of the ropes. "Now we've got to get the hell out of here!"

He grasped Kelly's hands, pulling her to her feet. She stood shakily, aching all over, her muscles stiff and sore. Brad put an arm around her waist and led her gently through the doorway, down the two flights of stairs to the hallway. As he hustled her past the dining room office toward the front door, Kelly glimpsed Smythe, crumpled facedown on the floor, and Clark Teague, slumped under one of the slatback chairs.

It wasn't until they were barreling down the graveled county road toward town that Kelly thought to ask Brad where they were going.

"To the police station, my love, to reassure Captain Creel. He actually seemed to be worried about you. Besides, I'm sure he'll be interested to hear that Mr. Teague goes in for abducting innocent citizens, tying them to bedposts, assault, battery . . ." As though struck with a chilling thought, he glanced quickly at her. "Did Teague . . . ?"

Kelly shook her head. "It was Smythe who threatened to — to see me later."

Brad let out a long relieved breath. "Well, he can see Captain Creel instead."

Captain Creel appeared genuinely glad to see Kelly alive and well. Whether he had been concerned for her safety or he merely felt relief at not having to search for another missing twin, she couldn't fathom. Abruptly his expression changed. Suddenly he flushed, gazing at her with the look of a trapped animal, as if wishing she'd vanish from sight and stop bothering him.

Without preamble, Brad said heatedly, "We're here to report an abduction. In fact, we intend to press charges . . . Kelly, tell him what happened."

At first Captain Creel listened with polite, reserved interest, but as Kelly went on, his face took on a cold, closed expression. When she had finished, he said, "That's a serious accusation, Miss Conover. Clark Teague didn't force you into his car, and we have only your word that this man Smythe abducted you.

"You claim you were held prisoner in the old mansion on the Alpenstock property. Right?"

Kelly nodded.

"I've known Clark Teague for a good

265

many years. He's a fine, upstanding citizen, and I've no reason to doubt his word. Now we'll see what *he* has to say about this."

The captain pulled a directory from his desk drawer, leafed through the yellow pages, picked up the phone, and dialed. In calm pleasant tones he said, "Clark, we have two rather overwrought and excited people down here who are talking about filing a complaint against you."

Kelly and Brad listened in tense, angry silence while Captain Creel related their story to Clark Teague. When he hung up, he leaned back in his swivel chair and regarded them with a baffled expression. "Clark Teague knows nothing whatever about all this." He paused to knock his pipe against the bowl of the onyx ashtray on his desk, then eyed Kelly narrowly. "In fact, he suggests that you made up this wild tale to get my attention, to force us to intensify the search for your sister."

Kelly blew up. "If he knows nothing about it, how does he know my sister is missing?"

Coolly, Captain Creel replied, "I imagine he's noticed that she hasn't been reporting for work in his office." He let out a patronizing sigh. "Everybody in town knows your sister is missing, Miss Conover. We're working on it, and when we find out anything, we'll let you know. Now let me give you a little friendly advice. Go home and get some rest — and give your imagination a rest as well. Don't make any more waves, Miss Conover."

Brad grabbed her left wrist and thrust it under Captain Creel's nose. "Look at this!" he shouted. "How do you think she got these burns?"

Coldly the captain replied, "I don't know how she got them, but they could have been caused by the straps on her ski poles."

For a long moment Kelly gazed at him, speechless. He believed Teague! He *wanted* to believe Teague! When at last she recovered her voice, she snapped, "Thank you very much, Captain Creel," and turned and stamped furiously out the door.

Brad, close at her side, took her arm and escorted her to the car. Once under way, Brad gripped the wheel in white-knuckled rage. When he spoke, his voice shook with anger and outrage. "Well, this really tears it. Now I know firsthand what they mean when they say 'You can't fight city hall'!"

"I'm not through fighting," Kelly said. "Not by a long shot!"

Brad reached over and patted her knee. "Good show!"

They rode for a while in silence, each

deep in thought. All at once Brad snapped his fingers. "I just remembered, while you were gone Eric called. He wants you to meet him as soon as you can on the beginner slope where he's teaching. Said he couldn't leave his classes, but he has to talk with you." Brad's tone betrayed a combination of mingled annoyance and suspicion that brought a smile to her lips.

"I wonder what he wants? Didn't he give you any idea?"

Brad gave what sounded suspiciously like a snort. "No, he didn't. From his tone of voice, I gathered it was very private, something he obviously didn't care to share with me, and he seemed in a hurry to ring off."

Kelly frowned. "I've no idea what it could be."

"*I* do!" said Brad in unmistakable tones of jealousy.

As if he hadn't spoken, Kelly went on. "If he wants me to meet him on the slopes, I suppose he wants to go skiing."

"It better damned well be *all* he wants."

Kelly laughed. "Don't be an idiot. You're forgetting he's in love with Kim."

"*I'm* not forgetting. I just hope *he* doesn't forget."

Kelly scowled. "You're forgetting you don't own me."

268

Brad swung down the dirt road to Alpine Village and pulled up before the chalet. He turned to look at her, smiling broadly. "The Indians or the Chinese or somebody believe that if you save a person's life, they are your responsibility forever."

She paused, thinking. It's true, he saved me, and thank God he did. But with his talk of Indian and Chinese beliefs, in effect running her life forever, the frantic feeling came over her that she was getting in deeper with him than ever before. Panicking, she thought, I've got to make a *break!*

Earnestly Kelly said, "I do appreciate your rescuing me from Clark Teague and his sidekick, don't think for a minute I don't! But I'm not your responsibility, now or ever." She took a deep breath, hating herself for having to hurt him, but it had to be said. "So while I go to meet Eric, you take the jeep and find yourself a place to stay."

Brad gave her a long, level look. She tried to read his thoughts and couldn't. At last he opened the car door and slid out. "Okay, my love. I can take a hint. I know when I'm not wanted. I'll find myself a room and go hunting for some snow bunnies."

Kelly gave him a swift, apologetic smile and slid into the driver's seat. "Happy hunting!"

Brad raised a hand to his forehead in mock salute. Raising one eyebrow he said, "If you're going skiing, you'd better take your skis." He slammed the door and strode up the walk. Kelly followed him inside and, without a word, picked up her gear and left.

Eric was waiting for her at the lift line, garbed in the Blue Angel ski togs that marked him as a ski school instructor. Kelly thought she detected an air of suppressed excitement, a tense, nervous look about his eyes, but the impression faded when Eric broke into a broad smile.

"Perfect timing," he said amiably. "I just sent the last novice packing it in."

Kelly returned his smile. "Good. What's this all about?"

Eric cast a quick look over his shoulder and took a step closer. "I don't want to talk about it here. You never know who's listening." His eyes lighted on her skis. "Since you came prepared to ski, let's ride the lift to the top and I'll tell you about it."

Seething with impatience and curiosity, Kelly stood with Eric in the lift line. While they waited their turn she told him about her futile search through the plats and her capture and release from Teague's dilapidated mansion.

When they were seated side by side in the lift, swinging high over the snowy face of the mountain, Kelly could contain her curiosity no longer. "Okay, Eric. What's happening?"

An exuberant grin lighted his face. "I've heard from Kim!"

Kelly gasped. "Is she all right?"

"She's fine . . . so far."

"What's that suppose to mean?" she asked anxiously.

"It means she can't come back to town. Not yet."

Kelly felt apprehension mounting inside her. "Why? Why can't she come back to town?"

Eric gave a helpless shake of his head. "You know Kim. She keeps her own counsel. She didn't say."

"Well, for heaven sake, Eric. Hurry up and tell me what she did say. Did she call you on the phone?"

Again Eric shook his head. "She mailed me a note — apologized for missing ski class and warned me not to tell anyone where she is. She said if you arrived before she got back to tell you she'll be home when all the trouble's over — soon, she hopes. At the moment it's too risky. She doesn't want you to get mixed up in all this . . ."

"But I *want* to get mixed up in it! I want to

help her! Where is she?"

"She's staying with a friend, Jill Adams, in a cabin on the far side of the mountain. Jill's a loner, too. Spends all her time weaving fabrics. Rides into town on her Honda every week to pick up mail and groceries."

"If Kim can't come here, I'll go to see her. Where is this cabin?"

Eric looked away, avoiding her intense gaze. "Sorry, Kim said not to tell anyone where she is, and I won't. I've already said more than I should, telling you about the cabin."

An angry flush suffused Kelly's features. "But you *know* me! I'm not her enemy, for God's sake!"

Relentlessly Eric shook his head, setting his jaw in a stubborn tilt. "Someone could follow you there; your friend Smythe could kidnap you again and force you to tell where to find Kim; you could get lost on the trails — you know how hard it is to find anyone who —"

"You could go with me!"

"No. The risk is the same for both of us. We could be followed —"

Kelly interrupted, determined to change Eric's mind. "We could bring her back here. I could protect her, help her settle this trouble, whatever it is."

Eric shot her a scornful glance. "You can't even protect yourself!"

She started to say they could demand police protection, but immediately thought better of it. Captain Creel's track record, doubting her word and siding with Teague, the town benefactor, left her little hope that he'd believe Kim needed police protection. Angrily she burst out, "You are the most stubborn man I've ever met!" Under her breath she added, "Next to Brad York."

Eric laughed. "The flip side of stubborn is adhering to principle — resolve."

Kelly made no reply. Her mind was wrestling with the problem of persuading Eric to take her to Kim.

Kindly, Eric said, "You need to cool down. How about a ski lesson" — he shot her an engaging grin — "as a peace offering. Okay?"

She shook her head. "The only thing I really want is to see Kim!" She cocked her head, looking up at him, a gleam of amusement sparkling in her eyes as if she were sharing an inside joke. "Besides, Brad told you I'm an expert skier — and I really am!"

"Really!" His tone was slightly ironic. "I've heard that before. Not to mention that Brad could be a bit prejudiced."

"I'm sure, on both counts," replied Kelly

lightly, thinking he was probably judging her own expertise by Kim's performance as a beginner. A last-ditch chance popped into her mind. Given a little time with Eric, maybe she could convince him that they should go after Kim. In challenging tones, she said, "I bet I can ski as well as you can. You choose the slope and I'll prove it."

An amused light glistened in his blue eyes, meeting the dare in her own. With a slight bow he said, "You make an offer I can't refuse. We'll try Silver Heels Run."

After riding the chair lift past the midstation to the top, they dismounted, skied down the ramp, and glided down a white-carpeted trail through a stand of dark spruce, emerging at the top of a run marked Devil's Descent.

"This looks like a terrific run," said Kelly enthusiastically. "Let's forget Silver Heels." She eased forward, leaning on her poles.

"No way." Eric nodded toward an orange plastic rope stretched between two stakes sunk in the ground from which fluttered tiny triangular orange flags and a sign: CLOSED. "It's closed because of an avalanche two weeks ago."

Kelly shaded her eyes with her hand and saw that a wide slide of debris — uprooted trees, rocks, and mud — had cascaded down the mountainside, leaving a raw, rock-strewn ridge.

"It's against the law to go down closed runs — far too dangerous." Eric moved on through the trees. "I think you'll find Silver Heels just as exciting and a lot safer."

Nodding assent, Kelly dug in her poles. Moments later Eric swooped past her down Silver Heels Run, leaving a plume of powder in his wake.

Kelly sailed after him, breathless, exhilarated, reveling in the feeling of freedom that swept through her as she flew down the steep mountainside on the long, tortuous run. Eric was right, Silver Heels was both challenging and exciting.

Kelly was unaware of the small plane droning overhead until they glided to a stop in a broad powdery basin. She looked up. The ski-equipped plane skimmed through the clear blue sky, trailing a long line of red letters. Her jaw dropped in astonishment as she made out the words: **BRAD LOVES KELLY!**

Kelly's heart seemed to loop with the plane. Brad's plane. She laughed aloud in delight. Only Brad York would think of declaring his love in sky-high letters for all the world to see!

Eric was laughing, too. "I think your friend Brad is trying to tell you something."

At his words, the significance of Brad's message struck her like a clap of thunder. Her smile faded. A fist seemed to close around her heart. "He's telling me good-bye."

A sympathetic expression came into Eric's eyes. "Oh, too bad he had to leave. I'm sorry."

"I'm not," said Kelly in choked tones. "I'm not one bit sorry." Even to her own ears, her words lacked conviction. Quickly she lowered her head so she wouldn't have to watch Brad flying out of her life forever. But she could still hear the drone of the plane fading away — a distance that widened with every passing sound.

Eric eyed her with a puzzled, speculative gaze. At last he said, "You look bluer than the Blue Angel logo! Since we're both batching it, let's make another run, then have dinner at the lodge."

Unable to speak over the tightness in her throat, Kelly nodded her assent.

It was shortly after ten when Kelly braked the Mustang to a stop before the chalet. A light gleamed behind the closed draperies. Brad had left the lamp on for her. She felt a sudden, twisting pain in the region of her heart. She jabbed the key in the lock, but before she could open the door it flew open, and a figure stood silhouetted in the light behind it.

"*You!*" cried Kelly, thunderstruck.

A low ripple of laughter filled her ears. "Were you expecting Santa Claus and eight tiny reindeer?"

Flabbergasted, Kelly shot back, "I'd expect to see them sooner than you!"

Brad smiled disarmingly and extended his hands in a helpless gesture. "Sorry to disappoint you, my love."

Her heart soared like a bird in flight. In facetious tones she said, "I suppose there wasn't a single room in town."

"Wrong! There was no gas in the jeep."

Kelly took off her outdoor things, dropped them on the couch. So he couldn't gather her up in a devastating bear hug, she crossed to the fireplace and stood with her back to him, warming her hands before the dying fire. He must have been waiting for her for hours. "Well, at least *I* have good news. Kim is holed up in some cabin on the other side of Blue Angel Mountain."

The next thing she knew, Brad's arms went around her, crushing her to him. "Kelly, that's great! Really great!" She whirled around and put her hands firmly on his shoulders, holding him away from her. Quickly she told him of her meeting with Eric. "So you see, I no longer need your help, and you can be on your way. In fact, I thought you were giving me a farewell buzz over the slope this afternoon."

Brad's brows rose in wonder. "Not at all. I was just keeping an eye on you and your self-appointed ski patrol. I didn't want you to forget me!"

A sudden mist clouded her vision. "It's not likely I'll ever forget you, Brad. Now it's time for you to go. So go climb in your old reliable superplane and fly home."

"Sorry, love. I never fly at night. You know that. It's one of my cardinal rules." He let her go, sank down on the couch, stretched out his long legs, and spread Kim's earth-toned afghan over him. Folding his arms behind his head, he closed his eyes.

It was true he never flew at night, thought Kelly, disconcerted. She gave him a long, appraising look. "Listen, Brad, you still don't understand. I'm going to try one last time to explain this to you." She sank down on the couch beside him. "All my life I've been tied to another person — Kim. True, we're what they call 'willing twins,' and we love each other dearly. But we've always been bound to each other. I want to experience life *un*bound."

Brad opened his eyes, gazing at her in astonishment. "You *are* unbound. Kim freed you when she bailed out to Blue Angel."

Kelly smiled. "Right. I want to keep it that way."

Brad took her hands in his. His voice was soft, persuasive. "Marriage is rather different from being half a twin. You see, in marriage, one and one are three. We can still be separate, but together we'll share a third life more fulfilling than each of us has apart." His lips curved in a smile so exuberant, so dazzling, it made her heart ache. "Yours, mine, and ours! We'll have it all, my love."

Softly she said, "I've had enough togetherness, Brad. I *know* what it's like to share a life with another person."

"You don't know what it's like with a *husband* person."

"And I'm not going to."

Brad let out a long sigh of defeat. "Okay. You win, sweetie. I hear what you're saying. Tomorrow I'll fly out of your life forever. I mean it."

Kelly let out a long sigh of relief. At last she'd gotten through to him. She tried to feel elated as well, but instead felt only a peculiar hollowness inside. "Okay, you can bunk here on the couch tonight."

"Right," Brad agreed, a little too willingly, she thought. "Kiss me good-night."

With a smile intended as a fond farewell, she bent her head to his. His lips, warm and tender, closed over hers. His arms went around her, holding her close against his chest. Softly he whispered, "Now I don't want you to worry about me, darling. I'll find someone new. They say there's someone for everyone, and somewhere out there there's a girl waiting — someone wonderful — waiting just to fall into my arms, into my bed . . . so don't worry, sweetie. This girl will love me like no one has ever loved me before."

Kelly, trying not to listen to his rosy predictions, heard instead a clicking sound — metal against metal — in the lock of the front door. "Brad," she exclaimed softly, "someone's trying to break into the chalet!"

Chapter Seventeen

Brad jumped up from the couch and strode to the door. Just as he reached it, it swung open. He fell on the intruder, hooked one arm under his chin, and with his free hand gripped an arm and wrenched it up behind his back. A terrified scream tore through the room.

Kelly leaped to her feet. For an instant shock made her speechless. Then she shrieked, "Kim! Kim! Oh Lord, am I glad to see you!"

At the same moment Brad, looking non-plussed, released his grip on the fragile intruder. Kim, clad in a red knitted hat, jeans, and jeans jacket, looking dazed and disheveled, slung her backpack to the floor and held out her arms to Kelly. "Lord, I'm glad to be here!"

After the first joy and excitement of their reunion had simmered down, Kelly made coffee and they sat in the warm glow of the firelight listening while Kim told them what happened.

"Well, the reason I came home," confessed Kim with a wry grin, "is that I saw Brad's message in the sky and knew you were both here. I knew then I'd have to come back." She glanced fondly at Kelly. "Knew you'd be worried sick about me, would turn the town upside down to find me, and I didn't want you to get mixed up with Clark Teague."

"Too late now," said Brad dryly.

Kim cast a startled look at Brad. "What happened?"

Kelly said, "Go on, finish your story first."

"Well, when I really got into tracking down our family, I found out that Clark Teague is selling property that doesn't belong to him. Conover property, for one."

Kelly's soft brown eyes widened in astonishment. "I thought Grandfather Conover had sold his section when he moved East."

"That he did. But there was other property as well. You see, Great-grandfather married Nellie Hill. Nellie Reimer Hill. The Reimer family settled here before the Homestead Act and staked out a claim of five hundred acres. If you trace the Reimer family, you'll find that Nellie was one of three children. She had a sister, Charity, and a brother, Joel. Charity and both their parents died in a smallpox epidemic when

Nellie was less than a year old, so a family named Hill took her to live with them. Nellie's brother Joel died in 1873, lost in a snowstorm."

"I saw his grave," Kelly said. "Lost while visiting his mine."

Kim nodded. "He'd inherited the property from his father, but he died a bachelor, which left our great-grandmother Nellie heir to her father's land at age thirteen. I suppose the Hill family paid the taxes to make sure Nellie hung on to the property, but when I tried to check it out, someone had made off with the pages in the tax book.

"It was when I was reading through some of the abstracts in the Alpenstock files that I became suspicious of Teague. I began going through the abstracts of Teague's land in the courthouse and found out Nellie Reimer Hill's property was deeded to a character named Teague. I finally caught on that Clark Teague was falsifying the records so it looked as if he owned half of Blue Angel Ridge."

Kim's eyes hardened and she clasped her hands tightly in her lap. "I couldn't let him get away with cheating all those people, but I knew there was no use trying to make a case against him in Blue Angel. He's a respected citizen — gives big donations to this and that. No one would believe me, especially old, loyal Captain Creel. He thinks Teague walks on water." She paused to catch her breath for a moment, but the anxious look in Kelly's and Brad's eyes made her continue. "So I watched and waited. When Jill Adams rode into town on her Honda, I collected a few files to prove Teague was bilking the public, dropped them in the mail to the state's attorney general, then took off with Jill to her cabin." A small, nervous laugh escaped her. "I'm sure Teague's been raking the mountain for me with a fine-tooth comb."

Brad let out a long, low whistle. "*Gunning* for you is more like it. At first he probably only wanted his records back. But by now I imagine he's heard from the attorney general. If he thinks there's a chance he'll be prosecuted, he'll want you out of the way so you can't testify against him in court. Honey, you're in big trouble!"

"I know. I'd planned to stay with Jill till the state took action. She picks up my mail at the P.O., you see, so all I had to do was wait it out until I heard from the attorney general." Kim shot Kelly a confident smile. "But I had to protect Kelly, and with the two of you here to protect *me*, I decided to come on home."

"Brad and I combed the mountain looking for you, too," Kelly said. "We thought you'd gone on a cross-country tour."

Kim shot her a remorseful smile. "I signed up, but I left town the day before the tour. I'm sorry I sent you off on a wild-goose chase. I didn't expect you here until the twenty-third . . ."

Brad laughed. "I made Kelly an offer she had to refuse, so she ran away to Colorado."

Kelly glared at Brad. "I did come earlier than we'd planned. First there were no letters from you. Then when I couldn't reach you on the phone, I knew you were in trouble. When I found you gone, I was frantic with worry, and to make matters worse, everywhere I went I met your enemies: Lauren Duval, Bill Smythe, Clark Teague. Even Eric was hostile till he found out who I was and why I was impersonating you."

"You were impersonating me! Good heavens, Kelly, you were really asking for trouble!"

Kelly grinned. "Would you believe? Yes, I guess you would!"

Kelly launched into an account of all that had happened while she was gone. Kim sat listening, first outraged, then angered over the trouble she had caused. When Kelly finished, Kim shook her head with an air of finality. "I can't go on letting people think you're me, letting you endanger your life. I'll have to make sure everyone in town knows I'm back."

"No!" Kelly exclaimed. "We're not going to risk *your* life either. I have a better idea. Instead of letting people think I'm you, we'll make them think you're me." She looked at Kim, appeal in her eyes. "It will mean a sacrifice on your part."

A determined glint came into Kim's eyes. "Name it."

"First thing tomorrow morning you drive over to the next town and have your hair cut and styled exactly like mine. Wear my clothes. When you get back, anyone seeing you will think you *are* me."

Kim nodded, almost cheerfully. "It might just work. Let's give it a go."

Early the next morning Brad drove to a nearby filling station and brought back a can of gas. Kelly and Kim stood outside the garage beside the jeep, watching while he poured it into the tank. "All systems go," he said cheerfully.

Kelly, glancing uneasily at the sky, heavy and overcast above the shrouded mountain peaks, hoped he was right. A storm appeared to be brewing. Brad had already forestalled any talk of his leaving, insisting he couldn't see the mountains in front of his face. Kim gave them each a quick kiss, climbed into the jeep, and roared away. Kelly and Brad stood waving her out of sight.

It wasn't until they returned to the kitchen, the cats hovering about their ankles, that Kelly noticed something wrong. "Brad, where's the white kitten?"

"Snow White? She's probably curled up on your bed. I'll take a look."

While Brad checked the bedroom, Kelly searched downstairs. Brad returned, looking baffled. "She's not in the loft."

"She's not here either," said Kelly worriedly. "She must have skinned out when we opened the garage door. I'll look in the basement."

Kelly flung a heavy sweater around her shoulders and ran down the basement stairs, calling the kitten. No white kitten bounded out to greet her, either in the basement or in the garage. She raised the garage door and raced outside, scanning the driveway and the road in back of the chalets straining to see the snow-white kitten against the white landscape. She started down the road, calling frantically. It wasn't until she passed a short stubby evergreen near the end of the road that she heard a faint mewling. Plowing through the snowbank at the side of the road she found the shivering kitten huddled in a mound of snow under the tree. "Come here, beast. You're too young to leave home!" She scooped up Snow White, tucked her under her sweater, and ran back to the chalet.

"Found her!" Kelly announced, bursting through the door into the kitchen.

Brad strode into the kitchen from the living room. "Good show, rescuing the runaway cat. By the way, someone from the ski school just called. Eric's class is having a special lesson this morning at ten and he wants Kim there."

"I wonder how he knew Kim was back."

Brad shrugged. "She probably called him last night after you were sacked in and I was in the shower."

"Why didn't he tell her then about his class?"

Brad grinned. "I imagine he was so bowled over that she was back, he forgot. Anyway, I said she'd be there. The class is meeting at Silver Heels Run."

Kelly shook her head. "She can't possibly be back in time. I'll give him a call so he won't worry when she doesn't show up."

Kelly disappeared into the living room and moments later returned to the kitchen. "Eric's already out on the slope. I tried to leave a message, but there was no one to take it to him. I'd better go in Kim's place. It'll give me a chance to alert him that Kim is going to look like me."

Brad bent down and kissed her on the lips. "You can tell him for me that this isn't happy hour — he's not going to get two for the price of one."

Laughing, Kelly reached up and grabbed his ears, shaking his head to and fro. "I'll tell him no such thing. I'll tell him, 'Double the pleasure, double the fun!' "

Kelly was somewhat surprised that Eric's class would be trying Silver Heels Run. It was an intermediate to advanced slope, and she had found it rather challenging yesterday.

Riding up the chair lift, she was further dismayed that everyone else got off at the first stage. Maybe Eric had reserved the upper slope for his morning classes. The expert skiers had probably gone to another area where there were more advanced runs to choose from. Still, someone from Eric's class should have been on the lift. Scowling, she glanced at her watch. No wonder. She was ten minutes late. No doubt Eric had drilled into his students that they must come to class on time.

Moments later she arrived at the top of the slope. A figure garbed in the puffy Blue Angel parka and ski pants worn by the ski school instructors waved enthusiastically to her. Strange, she thought, how they all look alike in those lodge ski togs. A sudden shaft of sunlight stabbed through a rent in the clouds, glinting off the mirror sunglasses he wore over his blue knitted mask.

Something struck her as odd. At once she knew what it was. Eric hadn't worn a ski mask yesterday. He'd told her he preferred to wear a bandana to protect his nose and chin. The mask gave him a totally different appearance, almost sinister. A feeling of foreboding flowed through her.

"Eric?" she shouted.

The man strode forward and an overpowering dread came over her. The man was not Eric. She would stay on the lift, she decided. But she'd made her decision a split-second too late. The man was beside her. Gripping her upper arm, he yanked her from the lift and pulled her down the ramp. Fear shot through her as she gazed about her and saw no one else.

Through stiff lips she said, "Where's the ski class?"

His voice, muffled by ski mask and scarf, was low and hurried. "You're late. They've gone on ahead."

In loud, accusing tones she blurted, "You're not Eric!"

Calmly, reasonably, he said, "Eric's gone on with his class. He asked me to wait for you."

Suspicion flared in her mind. He could be telling the truth. Admittedly she was more than a little hyper after her own ordeal, and all the anguish and turmoil over Kim. She'd go along to the run, and if she didn't see Eric's group on the slopes below, she'd take off.

The stranger tugged at her arm. "Hurry, or we'll never catch up with the others. I'll race you down." He swept off through the trees, glancing over his shoulder now and then as if to make sure she was following him. At last he drew to a halt at the top of a run.

Again Kelly glanced about her. She saw no marker bearing the name of the run, yet it looked familiar. The man stood at her elbow, waiting. "Let's go," he said quietly.

"In a minute," said Kelly. Stalling for time, she knelt down on one knee, pulled off her gloves, and adjusted the buckle on her left boot. From the corner of her eye she glanced to the right of the trail and saw nothing unusual. Her eyes flicked to the left. Several yards away, almost buried in the snow under a cluster of pines, she saw an ice-encrusted loop of orange plastic rope. Attached to it, barely visible, protruded a sign. All she could see were the letters: CLOS . . . She didn't need to see the marker to know this was Devil's Descent. Had he knocked down the rope, tried to hide the sign that warned skiers the run was closed because it was too dangerous? Clearly he planned for her to take off here and now! Her fingers trembled. She felt as though her blood were freezing in her veins. Kneeling on the other knee, she fiddled with the other buckle and lowered her gaze. The stranger stepped to her side. Just past the curve of the shining flat surface of his ski, in front of the binding, she saw engraved the initials C.T.

The warmth drained from her body. A tremor of fear coursed through her. On shaking legs she stood up. Taking a deep breath to steady her nerves, she dug in her poles. Nodding toward the run she said in dry, hoarse tones, "After you.

Chapter Eighteen

"After you," said Kelly again, more forcefully.

The man stood facing her, perfectly still, like an animal gathering itself to spring. Kelly could feel his eyes boring into her through his mirrored goggles but could read nothing of his expression. Had he followed her gaze, seen her freeze at the sight of the initials engraved on his skis? Summoning her courage she stared boldly back at the mirrored goggles. She couldn't let him see her terror.

Quietly he said, "You're too smart for your own good. But even an idiot can figure out that C.T. stands for Clark Teague." Kelly's throat closed. When she made no reply he went on in quiet, menacing tones. "You didn't fool me, bringing your twin sister in from New York. Smythe saw you last night, riding through town on that Honda. So all I had to do was pretend to be your beloved ski instructor." He gave a short, ugly laugh. "And now the novice skier is going to have a fatal *accident*." He lunged toward her, arms upraised, brandishing his poles.

At the same instant Kelly pushed off, plunging down the steep trail, sending up a plume of powder in her wake. She heard a muttered oath, the swish of skis as Clark Teague plunged downhill after her, terrifyingly close. She looked up and took a fast line to gain more speed, sweeping down the slope, swinging past snowy blue-green spruces and dark stands of fir in a death game of tag.

The sun had softened the top layer of snow, making it heavy and treacherous, like wet cement. She was flying down the steep slope at breathtaking speed, the wind biting her cheeks, whistling past her ears. She sped on, slipping, sliding, banking into a curve just in time to avoid a tree. Now and again she thought she was eluding her pursuer, but the next moment she could hear his skis hissing close on her heels, as though he would ski up her back. Never had a two-mile run seemed so long!

She rounded a bend and her heart leaped to her throat. Ahead loomed the mass of mud and debris, the smooth rock ledge left by the avalanche. She flew down the twisting, zigzag trail, desperately praying the mass hadn't shifted. Perspiration trickled down her face; every muscle in her body cried out. Breathlessly she negotiated a tricky hairpin turn, shifting her weight quickly to the left, right, then left again with lightning speed, and continued whizzing down the run.

A shout erupted in the bright, clear air. She dared not look behind her. She hugged the trail, curving to her right, and as she raced around three thick, towering spruces she heard a second shout, a long, drawn-out howl, like a creature in terror, or pain, that made her skin crawl. As she cleared the evergreens she glimpsed the giant ridge of mud and rock looming above her against the blue sky. Her breath caught in her throat. Flying through the air, arms and legs flailing, head over heels, like a pale blue puffy rag doll, was Clark Teague.

She schussed to a stop. Trembling with shock, she leaned on her poles. It wasn't hard to imagine what had happened. In her mind's eye she could see him zigzagging down the trail, coming suddenly upon the mass of debris, mud, and rock. Unable to shift his heavy bulk in time, his momentum had carried him forward across the slab of rock, propelling him through the stinging cold air into nothingness. Now he lay spread-eagle, motionless, in the long, broad, soft white basin below.

A feeling of nausea rose in her throat, mingled with loathing, repugnance, and something akin to pity. With an effort she closed her mind to the horror. Summoning all the strength and courage she possessed, she glided down to Teague's inert figure and came to a stop. He lay facedown, his face to one side, half-buried in the snow. His skis, automatically released from the bindings, lay nearby. Kelly bent down and with both hands scooped the snow away from his face. She pulled off a glove and forced herself to press her fingers to his neck, under the heavy curve of his jaw. His pulse throbbed under her fingertips. A born survivor, she thought grimly. She should try to bring him to, but she didn't dare touch him, didn't dare risk disturbing any broken bones. She would have to get help.

She stood up and glanced frantically about her. There was no orange call box from which to call the ski patrol. Setting her lips in a resolute line, she retrieved Teague's skis, crossed them, and stood them upright in the snow. Surely one of the skiers on the other slopes would spot the crossed skis and send help. She had just decided to leave Teague and go in search of a call box when she heard a plane in the distance. Shading her eyes with her hand, she scanned the wide blue sky. Moments later she saw a small red and white plane circling overhead. An exultant cry escaped her. "Brad's plane!"

Three hundred yards from where Kelly stood, the plane set down and glided up a slight incline, turned around, and stopped. Feeling as though she had wings on her heels, Kelly skied across the broad white basin toward the plane. The cockpit door burst open. Brad slid to the ground and enfolded her in his arms, crushing her tightly to his chest, his cheek pressed against hers. His voice was husky with relief. "Thank God you're safe! I've been out of my mind with worry!"

Shivering in the shelter of his arms, she said shakily, "Of course I'm safe! How come you're here?"

In low, tremulous tones he murmured, "When Kim got home, the first thing she wanted to do was call Eric to tell him she was back in town. She *hadn't* called him earlier! When Eric answered the phone I knew you were in trouble. You never saw a plane take off so fast in all your life."

Kelly gave a shaky laugh. "I'm glad you dropped by." She was distracted by a low roar, growing steadily louder. She turned from Brad and saw a yellow snow-cat mobile charging toward Teague's still form.

Following her astonished gaze, Brad said, "I radioed the police to get the hell out here — that there was going to be an accident. I knew it would be you or Teague." He grinned down at her. "I was betting on you to win."

Kelly smiled up at him. "You'd better believe it!" They stood watching while the ski patrol eased Teague onto a stretcher, loaded it behind the snow-cat, and roared away.

Brad shook his head. "I think Teague's had it with Alpenstock. He'll stand trial. Kim will testify and thereby do herself out of a job."

Kelly grinned. "I think Eric has another job in mind for her — a partnership."

"Not a bad idea, not bad at all," said Brad, nodding approval. As she watched, the smiling approval in his dark eyes faded, replaced by a serious expression. For a long moment he regarded her in somber silence. Finally he said, "Let's go home, Kelly."

Lightly, she said, "Not *home*, Brad, back to the chalet."

Wordlessly he motioned her into the plane.

When Kelly walked through the door of

the chalet, Kim hugged her tightly, tears of joy glistening in her eyes. When Kelly and Brad told her of Clark Teague's downfall, literally and figuratively, her relief matched their own.

Brad said, "Kelly and I will drive you into town and make a statement to the police, and I'm sure the state's attorney will pay a call on Teague before he leaves the hospital, so you're home free."

"I *feel* free as a bird let out of a cage," said Kim happily. "Poor Captain Creel will be so disillusioned with Teague. He'll be eating crow for weeks. And now if you two don't mind, I'll be off to tell Eric the good news." Within minutes they heard the jeep roaring down the road.

Brad zipped up his parka and picked up his baseball cap. "Well, I'd better be off, too."

"Off?" asked Kelly blankly.

"Yep." He shot her a knowing look. "I've been hanging around long enough. I've had a lot of time to think things over. All that's happened the past week has proved something. I've been kidding myself. I need you. But you don't need me. It's as simple as that." He raised one eyebrow, his lips curved in a wry smile. "You didn't even need me this morning — somebody else would have answered your signal. And Teague was the one who needed help, not you. You're in charge of your own life. I'm through badgering you, haranguing you to marry me. You're right when you say 'Marriage, who needs it!' You can get along without me very well."

Kelly felt her heart swell, as if it were about to burst. She rose from the couch and crossed to Brad. She had thought he was gone from her life on the morning he'd brought her the kitten. She had thought he was gone the day she was captured by Smythe. And she had thought he was gone when he buzzed the snow-clad basin while she was skiing with Eric. Three times she had sent him away, watched him walk out of her life, and each parting was harder than the one before. Each time she had felt an overwhelming joy that he was still here. This time, she knew in her heart he would never come back.

Putting her hands on his shoulders, she looked earnestly up into his face, meeting his gaze head on.

Softly she said, "I learned something this past week, too. I *can* get along without you very well, but I don't want to. I like having someone to come home to at the end of the day, someone to dote on, someone to dote on me. There's a long, lonely road out there, Brad. I don't want to walk without you, or ski without you, or live without you." She faltered for a moment. But the shining look in Brad's eyes made her go on. "Conover Executive Suites will never keep my heart warm." Her arms curved around his neck and she smiled lovingly into his eyes. "I'm ready to sign that lifetime contract." He gazed down at her with such love shining in the depths of his dark eyes that she wanted never to let him go.

"I've been ready, my love, since the day we met." His arms closed around her, his lips covering hers in a fervent kiss, their hearts beating as one.

After some little time she murmured, her lips brushing his warm cheek, "Brad, let's go home — home to New York."